Praise for

A ONCE AND FUTURE LOVE

"This is a wonderful, tender, poignant, and chivalrous tale that will captivate medieval fans everywhere."
—Romantic Times

"This is wonderful. It's one that grabs you, and at the end you say, Wow!"
—Bell, Book & Candle

"Anne Kelleher has written a beautiful story of timeless love. For a fascinating travel trip of your own, pick up *A Once and Future Love* and enmesh yourself in the historical detail and engaging love story."
—Romance Industry Newsletter

Jove titles by Anne Kelleher

THE GHOST AND KATIE COYLE
A ONCE AND FUTURE LOVE

The Ghost
and
Katie Coyle

Anne Kelleher

JOVE BOOKS, NEW YORK

HAUNTING HEARTS is a registered trademark of Penguin Putnam Inc.

THE GHOST AND KATIE COYLE

A Jove Book / published by arrangement with
the author

PRINTING HISTORY
Jove edition / November 1999

The Penguin Putnam Inc. World Wide Web site address is
http://www.penguinputnam.com

ISBN: 0-515-12703-5

A JOVE BOOK®
Jove Books are published by The Berkley Publishing Group,
a division of Penguin Putnam Inc.,
375 Hudson Street, New York, New York 10014.
JOVE and the "J" design
are trademarks belonging to Penguin Putnam Inc.

PRINTED IN THE UNITED STATES OF AMERICA

10 9 8 7 6 5 4 3 2 1

For Donny, my once and forever love

Prologue

1799

"The ship's going down!"

The anguished wail rose above the creak of straining timbers, carrying like a banshee's cry over the howl of the wind. Derry O'Riordan, tenth Earl of Kilmartin, looked up with glazed eyes at the man who tugged and pulled at the chains on his wrist on the other side of the dark, fetid cabin. He watched grimly as the other men around him surged to their feet, a writhing mass of unwashed flesh, blood-stained rags and clanking chains. The air reeked of sweat and fear.

"Open the hatch, you bastards!"

"Give us a chance to save ourselves, at least!"

"In the name of the Holy Mother, let us out!"

The cries rose to a fevered pitch as the ship tossed back and forth, rolling from one side to the other as easily as a cork thrown carelessly into a stream. A heavy body knocked Derry on his side. Splinters dug into his arm. There was a ghastly screech of cracking wood, and the ship rose to nearly a ninety-degree angle, hung suspended and crashed down once more. This time Derry heard shouts from the men up on deck.

The captives clung to each other and the floor searching for purchase. A few had their eyes closed tightly, their lips moving in silent prayer. Others screamed their prayers to Heaven, but most of the vocal ones cursed their fate loud and bitterly. Their voices rose as the lantern, the sole source of light, was extinguished in one mighty gust of wind that seemed to come from within the ship itself.

Derry rocked back on his heels, his chained wrists held before him. Curse the God who brought him to this place! It seemed like a waste of time, when he was so soon to meet the Maker, himself. Curses instead on his own head, and the foolhardy gesture of brotherly love that had brought him to this miserable end. Misguided fool that he'd been, he'd thought that taking his brother's place would enable him to serve out his brother's term of servitude, and allow his brother to care for the wife and child he adored, eventually enabling Derry to return to his native land, his lands and title safe from British interference. And to Annie, Annie, whom he'd glimpsed on another ship just as he'd been herded onto this one. Pray God she made it to Australia safely, she and the child she carried, the child he'd known at once was his. He'd thought she was dead, but the sight of her had only reinforced his determination to go on living. At least they were bound for the same place.

He bit back a howled curse at his own folly. He wasn't supposed to be on this slaver's ship, bound for

Van Diemen's Land. At least, he thought bitterly, he'd never know what it was to be a slave. But you'll never see home again, his mind screamed, so clearly Derry thought he must have spoken aloud. You'll never see Annie again—never know your child. The pain that clenched his heart was more acute than anything physical. He was about to be cheated forever of the life he was supposed to lead, the woman he loved, and the child that was the fruit of that love.

He struggled to his feet, even as the ship pitched and rolled violently on one side. He stumbled to his knees, and a falling timber fell squarely across his forehead. Lights exploded beneath his lids, and an unbearable pain burst from the back of his skull. A wave of water washed over him and he sputtered for breath. Dimly he felt the weight of the other men surging back and forth against him in the sudden deluge. *This is not justice,* he thought as darkness descended. *Annie, my love, I'll look for you in eternity, and I swear before God I'll never rest til I find you. Not in heaven and not in hell, and never beneath the waves. I'll search a thousand years if I must. But I'll find you, Annie, my love. I swear we'll spend eternity as one.*

Chapter One

1998

"This is ludicrous—I can't believe they expect you to live all the way out here in the middle of nowhere. What are you going to do when it snows?" Josh Gramby waved a dismissive hand at the tidy Cape Cods and neat stone fences that lined the Massachusetts country road.

Katie gripped the wheel of the car and gritted her teeth. He was being deliberately provoking. "Well," she said, as she downshifted around a curve, "I'm sure they have snowplows and salt trucks. And I guess if the weather is too bad, they won't mind if I cancel a class now and then. Geez, Josh. It's beautiful here. Why are you focusing on something that won't happen for months?"

Out of the corner of her eye, she saw Josh cock his blond head in her direction. "It's beautiful in Connect-icut, too. And when it snows in Manhattan, the whole city doesn't grind to a halt. And if the weather does get bad, at least in the city, you can get to the places you need to go. What if you get snowed in here?''

"Josh." Katie shook her head and one dark curl tumbled from the loose knot carelessly piled on top of her head. She tucked it behind her ear as she glanced once more in his direction. There was no use arguing with him. His broad face had that bulldog look on it—the one that meant he knew he was right and he was about to browbeat her into knowing he was right, too. ''We've been over this issue. I've accepted the job at East Bay and that's that. I'm going to live in the house they've assigned me and that's that, too. So there's no point in arguing about it.''

Josh rubbed a hand over his chin. He stared out the window at the passing scenery, and then turned back to her so quickly his starched blue oxford cloth shirt crackled. ''And what about us, Kate? What about our plans? I thought we were going to be together as soon as I finished law school and you finished that endless dissertation.''

Katie pressed her lips together and tried to concentrate on the road. She wasn't going to let him bother her. Josh and his starched shirts and his perfectly pressed khakis and his definite ideas about the way things should be usually made her feel safe and secure, but today he was making her feel smothered. He was so damn sure he knew what was right for both of them. Sometimes he seemed to forget that she was twenty-nine and had been on her own just as long as him.

Up ahead, she saw a huge pothole and swerved just in time to avoid it. Josh let out a loud sigh but said nothing. Katie pushed her sunglasses back up her nose.

It was hot inside the car, and her fair, freckled skin was covered with a light sheen of sweat. The country road wound up and down unexpected hills and around unexpected curves. Josh was right about one thing—this faculty housing did seem a bit out of the way. The campus was at least twenty minutes behind them. And even though the little town of East Bay was going to be her home for the next two years at least, the road made sightseeing, not to mention arguing, impossible.

She pointed to the directions that were written on a Post-it note stuck to the dashboard. "Can you read these, please? From that last stop sign?"

Josh slowly let out a deep breath. His displeasure was obvious, but he took the small yellow slip off the dusty dashboard and frowned at it. "Once past the stop sign, go another two point three miles on Mill Corner Road. Have you been watching the mileage?"

Katie nodded. "And we're just about at two point three now. What next?"

"Watch for the iron gates on your right—there's a mailbox with a red flag and the number on your left." Josh peered out the window. "There—isn't that a red flag on a mailbox now?"

Katie slowed, peering to her right. "Oh, yeah...." Her voice trailed off as she saw blue shingles and two minivans parked in the driveway. She glanced at Josh. "That wasn't it. And you know it."

"Every mailbox has a red flag. What kind of landmark is that supposed to be?"

She pursed her lips and mentally counted to ten. He wasn't going to spoil this for her. He just wasn't. "Josh, I know you're upset that I'm not moving in with you right now—"

"Kate, if you don't want to live with me, that's fine. I just don't understand why you can't find something in your field closer to the city. Are you trying to tell me that the only job in Irish Studies on the entire East Coast is in some out-of-the-way nowheresville in Massachusetts? I thought Columbia offered you—"

"Columbia offered me a research assistantship. Not a teaching job. And it wasn't in Irish Studies—it was in the Lit Department. And yes, there's another position in Irish Studies available—in South Carolina. Would you prefer it if I'd gone there?"

"Damn it, Kate, you know what I mean. I thought we would be together once you were finished—" He hesitated for a split second, but his disdain was clear.

"Playing around?" she shot back. Instantly she felt ashamed. There was no point in continuing to argue with him. She'd made up her mind, and his refusal to accept her decision was making her increasingly angry. Now she wished he'd stayed in Manhattan, or Fairfield, or wherever he liked.

"I never said that."

"You never had to." The car bounced violently over another pothole and the boxes piled on the backseat jounced up and down. Katie braced herself for the sound of shattering glass. But she heard nothing, and they drove on in silence.

She tapped the brake as she noticed a red flag, barely recognizable, rising from a mass of leafy vines. She understood immediately why Fran, the secretary at the college, had mentioned the red flag so specifically. It was the only way to be sure the object beneath all the leaves was a mailbox. The late afternoon sun glinted on dull brass numbers. She slowed nearly to a stop and looked to her right. Massive iron gates rose out of a nest of ivy and vines and crumbling stone walls. The gates were covered in peeling black paint, but they stood open as if in welcome. A graveled drive led down a gentle slope.

"I think this is it."

Josh sighed loudly. "Let's go see the place."

Katie turned the wheel. The car moved down the driveway's incline, as hanging branches brushed against the hood and scraped against the sides.

"Good thing you didn't get that new car after all, Kate. You'd spoil the paint in this jungle."

Katie bit back the retort that rose to her lips. She peered through the verdant foliage that grew lush and thick on both sides of the drive. It was impossible to guess how wide the drive really was, for the trees and shrubs that lined both sides were so badly overgrown. A leafy branch intruded into the open window and she brushed it aside, but not before she caught a whiff of its fragrant green scent. "Mmm," she smiled, "that's nice." Next to her, Josh only rolled his eyes. "Fran said the house hasn't been occupied since last April. I guess no one's been out to cut the trees back, either. But it's beautiful, Josh—don't you agree? Look, it's like a green aisle."

She gestured with one hand. Shafts of afternoon sunlight streamed through the overhead branches. The whole drive was suffused with a gold-green glow. "And smell that—you can smell the ocean—and flowers— there must be an herb garden somewhere close."

Josh said nothing. Katie guided the car down the drive. Ahead two pillars, made of fieldstones about ten feet tall, rose on either side. They were topped with cracked stone urns. Ivy spilled out of the urns, and twined around the pillars. "Now—the house is on the right—" She broke off, speechless at the sight that lay before them.

A fieldstone cottage nestled on top of a low hill. The front door and a wide bay window overlooked a large pond. Katie stopped the car. "Look, Josh—just look how beautiful it is."

She got out, heedless of his reaction. All around her the air was moist and green with the scent of the water. She heard the trickle of running water and looking around, realized they were parked on a bridge. The bridge spanned a brook, which ran into the pond. On both sides, low stone walls were covered with ivy and wisteria vines. Katie slammed her door shut. The pond lay deceptively still in the sun. Then a fish leapt from the surface and dove down again with a loud splash. Katie followed the trace of a footpath, mesmerized. She had never expected anything like this. A stone bench was positioned on the opposite side of the pond beneath the drooping branches of an ancient willow. The grass was short, and newly mown piles of clippings lay haphazardly on the lawn between the house and the pond. Giant rhododendrons hugged the walls of the cottage and spilled over the low stone walls that separated the house from the woods. Katie walked a little closer, her sandals silent on the thick grass, and saw rock gardens gone to ruin. The tangy scent of herbs greeted her as she passed by, and she saw thyme and oregano, rosemary and lavender. Bees buzzed contentedly among the heavy purple heads.

"Look at this, Josh," she said, more to herself than to him. "Can you believe this place?" There was something magical about it. It was like an enchanted island in the middle of the forest, she thought, a place where fairies came to dance under the light of the full moon, a place where deer would come to drink in the cool of a summer dawn.

"No, I can't believe it at all." His polished penny loafers crunched across the gravel of the drive. "This place is a mess."

"A mess?" She turned to face him in disbelief. "It's not a mess—it's beautiful. It's wild and wonderful and . . ." She paused, searching for words. Despite the fact that it was so overgrown, the place made her feel as though it had been waiting for her. She felt welcomed and protected. She spread her arms wide. "This is one of the most beautiful places I've ever seen. It just needs someone to take care of it." She stopped, startled. She hadn't expected to say that. She hadn't even been thinking that, when she'd started to speak. Where had that thought come from? But the more she thought about it, the more it seemed to be true. Pond House desperately needed someone to take care of it—someone to clip back the vines and prune the trees and weed the herb beds. And plant flowers and cut the rhododendrons back—images of gardening catalogs flashed through her mind. She could imagine what her mother and her twin sister, Meg, would say when they saw the place. They'd have trowels and shears in their hands before they even set foot in the house.

Suddenly she felt a rush of energy and her mood, which had been weighed down by the conflict with Josh, lightened. "Come on." She reached for his hand and smiled at him. "Let's go see the house."

He allowed her to drag him over the lawn past the pond and over the footbridge. On the bridge she gasped once more. "Look—there's a little waterfall and another pond." A shallow stream of clear water spilled over the edges of a rock ledge. Dark-green watercress grew on the banks, and yellow butterflies darted in the long leaves of orange lilies clustered by the bridge. "I can't believe how beautiful it is," she murmured.

Josh said nothing. He was staring at the woods on the far side of the pond, where another stream flowed out and disappeared into the trees. "I guess the beach is that way." He raised his hand as if to point, then stopped and frowned. "Wait a minute. There's someone in those trees watching us. Hey—you there!"

Katie squinted at the trees and saw nothing that even remotely resembled a person. The dark trunks and leafy branches blended into a seamless crazy quilt of all shades of green and brown. Anything even remotely human would stand out against such a backdrop. She rolled her eyes. "Cut it out, Josh. You're not going to scare me like that. And besides, maybe there's a path through there that goes down to the beach. So what if you saw someone walking through the woods?"

"He wasn't walking. He was right against that tree"— Josh pointed—"right over there. He was watching us."

Katie shook her head, and in that moment a flash of white against the shadowed greens caught her eye. "So someone was passing through and stopped to look. So what? The beach must be close by—I can smell the salt air. Come on, let's go look at the house. Do you have the key?"

Josh nodded. "Yeah. You'd better let me try first." He shot one more look in the direction of the woods, and walked away, muttering, "vagrants" under his breath.

She followed him up the flagstone walk, determined to ignore his bad humor, marveling at the tiny purple flowers clustered around the stones. The whole place seemed to pulse with energy, rich and dense and green. The light was intense, an even golden glow in the late afternoon. What must the place look like in the morning, she wondered. She waited, trying to curb her impatience as Josh fiddled with the lock.

"What's wrong?" she asked when she heard him swear under his breath.

"I can't believe you think you're going to manage out here, Kate. How are you ever going to open the goddamn door?" With a grimace, Josh turned the key in the lock and shoved the door open.

"Maybe"—she stepped past him over the threshold—"maybe I just won't lock the door."

Josh groaned, rolling his eyes to the ceiling. He handed her the key, then wiped his hands on a handkerchief he pulled from the back pocket of his khakis. He wiped his hands as deliberately as if he'd touched something dirty. Katie slipped the key inside the pocket of her jeans, paused just inside the door and smiled with delight.

"Look," she said, more to herself than to Josh, "Look how beautiful it is, Josh."

"I wish you'd stop saying that," Josh said. He reached for the wall switch, jiggled it, and snorted. "Not even a goddamn lightbulb. And I wish you'd stop saying that word."

"Which one?"

"Beautiful."

Katie glanced at Josh over her shoulder as she walked further into the room. A wide bay window looked out over the ponds and the waterfall, and through the panes of glass, it was possible to hear the babble of the water over the stones. A low couch, covered in cheap imitation brown leather, faced the window, and before it, a coffee table with battered legs and a ring-scarred top stood on a scrap of threadbare red rug. An ancient floor lamp with a yellowed shade had been left in the corner near the window. A huge fireplace filled one wall. Sunlight streamed through windows on the opposite side of the room, and through a doorway, Katie could see a cozy white kitchen.

Katie turned around, staring. The place smelled of fresh paint. If the outside had been neglected, at least the university had seen to the upkeep of the interior of the cottage. The wooden floors gleamed, the brass and-irons by the fireplace shone. Even the windows looked as though they'd been freshly washed. The furniture might be sparse and cheap, but it looked clean. "I don't understand you, Josh. This place is beautiful and you know it. I'll have plenty of peace and quiet to work on my application for the Clancy grant I was telling you about. Can't you be happy for me?"

Josh didn't answer. Instead he walked into the kitchen. "There's a bad smell in here, Kate. You'd better get someone out here to check the drains."

It was Katie's turn to roll her eyes. "Yes, Josh. First thing." She followed him to the kitchen, where a tiny table with two rickety white chairs had been pushed into a corner. She sniffed. "I don't smell anything but fresh paint. And look, at least I'll have a place to eat."

"I think it's coming from over here—probably from the sink. Something must have crawled in one of the drains and died. And I'd think twice about sitting in one of those chairs. They look like they've been here since World War Two.''

Katie came closer, sniffing. ''I still don't smell a thing. And try to be nice, Okay?''

Josh shook his head. ''Okay. It's just me, then.'' He yanked open a drawer. ''Probably mice in here.''

''Josh!'' Just as Katie spoke, the drawer seemed to jerk away from Josh's grip. He gave a startled cry, and then a louder one. The drawer slammed shut on his fingers. ''Are you okay?''

''Damn,'' he muttered, rubbing his fingers together. ''What a dump. Must be a truckload of grease on that. You'll have roaches for sure.''

''Maybe it's the ghost.'' Katie winked. ''Fran said this place had a history—whatever that means.''

''Probably it means nobody can stand to live here once it starts to snow.'' Josh shook his head and stalked out of the kitchen, leaving her to cast an appraising eye around the small room. The white appliances were all at least twenty years old or more, but very clean. They looked to be in good repair. The floor was black-and-white squares, and the windows were bare. Katie imagined red-and-white-checked gingham curtains. She gingerly leaned against one of the chairs. It appeared to be more sturdy than it looked. She smiled once more, thinking she would have to make a list of things to buy, when she heard Josh yell again.

She followed the sound down the narrow hallway, until she came to the tiny blue tiled bathroom. ''What happened?''

He pointed to shattered glass, strewn all over the countertop. ''That's what happened. I touched the god-damned light switch and the next thing I know, the whole bulb's exploding. I don't think this place is safe, Katie. The wiring, the plumbing—I think the house needs a complete overhaul. It's just been vacant too long. Why don't you let me drive us back to town? I don't like the feel of this place and I don't like the thought of you living here. We'll find a nice place to stay the night, and in the morning, you go tell them you want something better to live in.''

"And if they don't give it to me—quit?" Katie crossed her arms over her chest.

"Sure. That sounds like the smartest thing you've said all day."

Katie bit back a retort. She mentally counted to ten, then said, "It probably is a good idea to have everything looked at, Josh. But the electricity's working fine. I heard the refrigerator. And I didn't smell anything in the kitchen at all, so I doubt there's much wrong with the plumbing, either. I think you're just imagining things because you don't want me to stay here."

Josh pursed his lips. "You're right, Kate. I don't like the idea of my girlfriend staying in some ramshackle cabin in the middle of nowhere when she could be staying with me in a brand new co-op in Manhattan. Or a nice apartment in Fairfield, close to stores and schools and—"

"Oh, Josh," Katie sighed. She looked at him sadly. How was it possible they'd been together for the last three years? "You sound like a real estate agent. Don't you understand? I want to stay here. You're right—the house has been empty a long time, and the grounds are a mess. But I'll be spending most of my time on campus, don't you see that? I want this job—I'm really thrilled to be here. Can't you try to be happy for me?"

"Happy for you, Kate?" He pushed past her, his feet crunching over shards of glass. "It's kind of tough to be happy when my girlfriend is going to be a four- or five-hour drive away. You know there's no way I'm going to be able to get up here. They're going to expect me to bust my butt, especially the first year. And once the winter starts, you aren't going to be able to get down the goddamn driveway, let alone I–95. How often do you think we're going to see each other?"

"But, Josh, we've been apart before. All the summers I spent in Dublin—"

"And you think I liked it?" Josh shook his head. "You just aren't hearing me, Kate. You wouldn't be the first woman to put her career on hold to establish a family."

Katie swallowed hard. What was he saying? "Are you telling me you want to get married? Start a family?"

Josh shrugged. "Well, maybe in a year or two. After I've got a couple years under my belt at Tyler, Harris. In the meantime—"

"In the meantime, why can't I do what I want to do?" Katie stared up at him. His jaw was clenched and he wasn't looking at her. He was staring down at his shoes, now heavily coated in grass clippings. Her own feet, practically bare in strappy sandals, were clean. Suddenly she felt very sad. Three years was a long time. She tried to remember if he'd ever acted this way before. He'd always been opinionated, and she often gave in rather than argue. But she wasn't giving in now. And if it meant that their relationship had come to an end, so be it.

She took a deep breath. "Will you help me bring my stuff in?"

"Yeah," he said. "Sure." Without another word, he walked down the hall and out the door.

Katie looked around. Shards of broken glass sparkled like diamonds on the tile floor, the countertop and in the sink. What if that had happened while she was getting out of the bath? She shivered. Josh was probably right about one thing, at least. She should insist that the university send someone out to go over the place. Living alone out here could be dangerous. And she didn't like unexpected surprises. At least, not unpleasant ones. A cool breeze ruffled her bangs and she suddenly noticed that the window was open a fraction of an inch. As she placed her fingers on the sash to shut it, a big brown spider dropped from above. It landed on the back of her hand.

She gasped, more surprised than frightened, and the insect scuttled away. That was nasty, she thought. And fleetingly, she wondered what other surprises Pond House might have in store for her.

The car slipped down the long driveway into the fading afternoon, disappearing beneath the trees. In one fluid motion, the tall man stepped out from the shadows of the oaks. They were ancient; unlike so much in the world he found himself in, the trees were one thing that had been there even before he'd arrived. He padded over the moss-covered ground, slipping silently over the bridge. He drifted toward the house. The August afternoon was warm, and through the newly opened windows he could make out the boxes that contained the young woman's possessions.

The young woman. Emotion surged through him.

Could it be true that Annie had returned to find him? He was trapped—caught in the flow of some energy field that emanated from the Stones within the forest. But her soul was free—could it be that after two hundred years, she'd finally come back to him? That same face— that upturned nose, and huge dark eyes framed by long thick lashes and delicately arched brows. He hadn't been able to get close enough to see if she had the freckles he'd loved to kiss. But he'd seen clearly as day the lush waves of her upswept curls and the slender lines of her body beneath the outlandish clothes.

Hope swelled, and just as quickly another emotion rose to crush it. Fate had played more than one cruel joke upon him—why should he think the woman's resemblance to Annie could be anything else? The accumulated pain of two hundred years of longing crashed over him.

But who was she? he wondered as he gazed from box to box. A colorful swirl of fabric peeked out of one, a statue's slender arm from another. Most, though, appeared to be labeled "books." Who was this woman who so resembled Annie, and seemed, if the glimpse of her possessions was any indication, so completely her opposite. Annie, to his knowledge, had never read a book in her life. Or maybe she had, he mused. Who knew what her life had been like in Australia? Who could tell him? The silent boxes taunted him with their secrets, tantalizing as the face of the newcomer. Unlike the other occupants of Pond House, most of whom had come and gone almost without his notice, this woman had definitely caught his attention. Who was she? Was there any other connection to Annie besides the physical resemblance? And what did her arrival mean? Musing, he drifted back across the lawn, over the bridge, and slipped back into the shadows beneath the trees to await her return.

Chapter Two

The last rays of the setting sun lent the living room a warm glow as Katie opened the last of her boxes. The movers were bringing the rest of her possessions tomorrow—or so they'd assured her, at least. She didn't have enough to comprise a full load, and so she'd had to wait until they had another household moving to the same area. Fortunately, the meager furnishings of Pond House were all she really needed for the moment.

She rocked back on her heels, sorting quickly through the contents of the box. It contained her copies of the texts she had decided to use for her first semester survey course of Irish literature, and the notes from a couple of her graduate courses. As she lifted the yellowing sheets of paper from the dog-eared folder, a random breeze blew through the window, scattering the pages. She scrambled after them. Her notes were too precious to misplace. Sitting cross-legged on the threadbare rug, she shuffled them back into order lovingly. Had Josh always been so dismissive of her work? The history and the language and the literature of Ireland from the arrival of the Tuatha De Danaan to the most recent troubled times had always held an endless fascination for her.

For Katie, heroes lived in the pages of Irish lore, from Finn, the fair-haired giant who'd founded the Fianna, the elite company of warriors who guarded the borders of Eiru, to Oisian, who lived among the "Other," to Hugh O'Neill, the fighting Prince of Donegal, who'd gone into exile rather than live in defeat, to Redmond O'Hanlon, the outlaw who'd ridden into history from some of Ireland's darkest years. An outlaw rapparee. Unbidden, the words of a song ran through her mind:

My spurs are rusted, my coat is rent, my plume is damp with rain . . .
But my rifle's as bright as my sweetheart's eyes, my arm is strong and free . . .
What care have I for your king or laws, I'm an outlaw rapparee . . .

An image of a tall, blue-eyed, dark-haired man clad in tight dark breeches, a billowy white shirt, and a plumed hat rose before her, and fleetingly, Katie wondered what it would be like to be that outlaw's sweetheart. She laughed aloud as another gust from the window brought her back to the present. Silly fantasies. No wonder Josh didn't take her work seriously. She rose to look out the window, thinking she'd always been a sucker for blue eyes. Blue eyes had been one of Josh's main attractions. She drank in the lush view, now bathed in a purplish twilight. A cat was curled up on the footbridge, sound asleep. Sleep, she thought. That sounded like a plan.

She dismissed the thoughts of Josh, and firmly set aside her daydreams. It would be easy to lose herself that way here, she thought. She sighed once more, and this time she caught the faintest hint of a scent, sweet and spicy and pungent, an old-fashioned scent she thought she recognized but could not immediately place. She breathed in again, and this time the fragrance was gone. There must be a hundred scents out there, she thought, as she watched the water flow across the wide rocks. Suddenly, she felt as though someone was standing next to her. She whipped around, half-expecting to see—*to see what, you silly goose,* she scolded herself. Oisian? Hugh O'Neill? Redmond O'Hanlon?

She shook her head. Enough nonsense. Focus, Katie, focus. She really needed a desk. She'd never be able to organize her materials without one. The Clancy grant would mean recognition on an international scale, if she were lucky enough to win it. But she had to get organized, if she was serious about applying for it. She would have a lot to do this semester, and the application would never be ready by the January fifteenth deadline if she didn't get busy.

She glanced around the room, assessing where to put her bookshelves, and wondering if she had enough. Already she could visualize things she wanted to buy. If she wasn't careful, she'd spend her entire first semester's pay furnishing the house the way it should be furnished. The way it wanted to be furnished. Immediately she was struck by the oddity of that thought. The idea that a house would *want* to be furnished in some way or another . . . well . . . she shook her head. It had been a long

day, and the argument she'd had with Josh had only
made it seem longer.

The thought of Josh made her suddenly depressed.
She wandered into the tiny kitchen and opened the refrigerator before she could stop herself. Some habits died
hard. Katie'd been a chubby child, and now, daily ex-
ercise was a part of her routine. It helped maintain her
size eight figure. But when the going got tough—the
tough went out to eat, as her mother liked to say with a
laugh.

Katie shut the door. Suddenly she felt very much
alone. Meg was in Dublin, which might as well have
been the moon. And the rest of her family, all in Phil-
adelphia, seemed a million miles away. The telephone
company was coming tomorrow to install a new line,
and she wished she'd remembered to include a phone in
the boxes she'd brought with her. A friendly voice
would be welcome right now. And as for Josh—she
pushed the thought of him out of her mind. He'd left
right after she'd driven him back to campus, promising
to call her. But he didn't know her new number, and
somehow she didn't think she'd be calling him any time
soon to give it to him.

She realized how tired she was—too tired to eat any
of the food she'd bought after dropping Josh off. She'd
take a hot bath, have some warm milk, and go to bed.
There were three bedrooms in the house, and each contained a double bed and a dresser. Katie had appropri-
ated the largest of the bedrooms. She'd bounced on the
mattress a couple times, and it seemed comfortable
enough.

She wandered into the bathroom, and cast a quick eye
around, searching for the spider. But it was nowhere to

be seen. She turned the taps of the tub. Anxiously she watched the water run, looking for any kind of discoloration, but the water looked fresh and clear. She uncorked a vial of bubble bath she'd been saving in her travel kit and poured it under the flowing spigot. As the fragrance rose on the clouds of steam, she sighed. She pulled her T-shirt over her head, and stepped out of her jeans. She brushed out her hair, the thick, dark curls wild and unruly in the humidity. As she piled her hair back into a loose knot on top of her head, a cool breeze made a chill go down her spine, and raised gooseflesh on her arms.

She looked at the window with a start. It was open again—she knew she'd shut it. Maybe Josh must've opened it—he'd used the bathroom before he left. She shut it again, firmly. The bathroom window overlooked the pines that bordered the cliff. Somewhere beneath those branches was the path that led down to the beach. She would have to explore the property tomorrow.

She slipped out of her underwear and stepped into the hot water. There was nothing wrong with the water heater, that was for sure. The water was so hot it turned her flesh pink on contact. She settled back with a sigh, and closed her eyes. The scent from the water filled her nostrils, and she thought she caught a whiff of the same scent she'd smelled in the living room—that peculiar pungent spicy fragrance. She breathed in deeply just as the light over the sink flickered. Katie sat up, peering anxiously at the fixture. She'd replaced the bulb as soon as she'd cleaned up the glass, and it had seemed to work fine. She waited a few minutes. The light shone steadily. She sank down into the water, leaned back against the tub and closed her eyes. It was nothing. Josh had her head filled with all sorts of maintenance nightmares.

His attitude in general had surprised and saddened her. How could he have so dismissed her passion? There had never been anything else she'd wanted to study so much, and working on her degrees had been the easy part. Finding a job had been nearly impossible. How could Josh fail to understand how lucky she was to have landed this one? Academic positions weren't exactly a dime a dozen. She needed to establish herself in the field, and this was her first opportunity to do so. And if she could win the Sean Seamus Clancy Award . . .

The light flickered again. She sat up with a sigh. Okay, Okay, she thought. I'll call the university tomorrow—as soon as I have a phone. She got out of the tub and toweled herself off, peering out the window. Except for the steady chirp of insects, the night was still. The leaves drooped on their branches and there was an almost expectant hush about the place. Even inside the house, she could feel it—something waiting, whispering a temptation to join it, to come dabble her toes in the waterfall's rush, to pluck the purple heads of the lavender and rub the essence over her body, and dance on the plush green grass by the light of the moon. For a moment she considered going outside, but a wave of weariness overtook her. There would be plenty of time to explore tomorrow. And all the days after that.

She padded into her bedroom, tugged her nightgown over her head and suddenly felt so tired she wanted nothing more than to lie down and sleep. She was just settling into a comfortable position when she thought she heard a voice—a man's voice, low and yet distinct, calling in the night. She sat up, cocked her head and listened. For the briefest moment, she felt a stab of fear.

But she heard nothing more. It was her imagination, she decided. Between coming to East Bay, arguing with Josh and moving into Pond House, it had been a full day. No wonder she was hearing things. It was an owl, most likely, hooting at the moon. With a yawn, she snuggled into her pillow and fell fast asleep.

Beneath the midnight moon, Derry faded back into the trees. He ought to feel like a cad for staring at the woman so blatantly, so boldly, but he'd known he was invisible. And this wasn't just any woman—this was someone who reminded him of Annie so powerfully it reverberated through every aspect of his being.

He'd been drawn to the sight of her as she'd moved through the house—the sound of the half-forgotten tunes she sang beneath her breath—and the lines of her face, and the shape of her jaw. She wasn't exactly Annie. He'd seen it at once when she'd shrugged away her clothes. Where Annie's body had been lean and hard and almost boyish from a life of deprivation and struggle, this woman's hips and breasts were lush and rounded, although her waist was slender enough to tell him she'd most likely never borne a child.

With a sigh, he stepped back within the center of the vortex of energy. The energy sustained him in some way, he knew, even as it prevented him from moving too far from its center.

"Help me!"

The familiar cry shattered the still night, echoing through the forest. Derry stiffened. He wasn't the only form of energy trapped by the Stones. His own voice calling for help when he'd died back there on the frozen path often replayed itself again and again. There were other echoes in the night, too, of course, and other shapes drifting and fading beneath the trees, but they had considerably less substance than he for some reason he had not fathomed in two hundred years. Somehow, the essence of his existence was more tangible, more concrete, than the shadows that slipped between this world and the next. They were only echoes of sights and sounds and smells from another time, trapped by the constant flow of the energy that emanated from the earth. He, alone, it seemed, was trapped in this curious in-between existence, not quite of this world, nor yet of the other, and it was a puzzle with which he'd grappled since he'd watched his body be carried from the beach two hundred years ago.

In two hundred years, he'd yet to understand the mysteries of Pond House. And now it seemed it had added yet another. There had to be some reason for this woman's presence. He'd slip inside Pond House the next time he saw her leave the property. It would give him a chance to discover more about her. He couldn't help but hope that her arrival had some meaning for him. And if there was a way, any way at all, that he could find out what it was, he intended to discover it. As soon as he possibly could.

Chapter
Three

Katie stepped past the wide-flung French doors of the reception hall and leaned against the stone railing of the balcony. The late-afternoon sun glowed like a red Christmas tree ball just above the highest trees. It was going to be warm again tomorrow. Inside, she could hear the babble of voices and the clink of glasses and plates. She drew a deep breath. Maybe Josh hadn't been entirely wrong, after all. With few exceptions, her new colleagues were notable only for their polite distance. The reception to welcome new faculty was only supposed to last two hours, but this first hour had seemed at least twice as long as that. Her head ached from the tension of trying to socialize with strangers, and she was tired from the long day of moving. But she'd been determined to seem eager and cheerful and glad to be here. It was so important that she make a good impression. If she didn't Josh might yet get his wish. She wasn't sure she'd last for more than one semester.

So many new faces, so many new names. She sighed so loudly she startled herself. Terence Callahan, the dean of interdepartmental studies, was clearly in her corner. He'd gone out of his way to introduce her around. And to be fair, most of the people she'd met from the History and English Departments seemed friendly enough, if a little distant. She was the only new member in either department, and that made it a little harder to break the ice. Carolyn Holt, the chairman of the History Department, seemed marginally interested in her work, and Terry Callahan was as grandfatherly as she remembered from her interviews.

Unfortunately, the one who'd been the most hostile was also the person she needed most to impress. Reginald Proser, chairman of the English Department and her immediate boss, had made it quite clear that he regarded the whole idea of interdisciplinary studies as "dilution of the disciplines." She understood all too well what the pompous little man meant by that. He was afraid his department budget would be cut to make room for faculty whose expertise crossed a number of department lines.

Terry Callahan had taken pains to assure her that Proser's chilly greeting had nothing to do with Katie personally. Katie was still nervous. Proser had been on sabbatical in England when she'd come for her interviews, and she wasn't sure she'd have accepted the position if she'd known about his hostility. As her department chair, Proser wielded a fair amount of power over her future at East Bay.

Katie rubbed her temples and gazed out over the green quad. Ivy-covered buildings rose on either side, each no more than three or four stories. East Bay was only about fifty years old, but the architecture made it look as if it dated back to Tudor England. Maybe Josh was right. Maybe this was just a pretentious little place filled with pretentious little people. Maybe she shouldn't have been so quick to turn Columbia down.

"Had enough punch and cookies?"

The deep masculine voice startled her out of her reverie, and she jumped, knocking her knee against the high stone railing. "Ow!" she cried out involuntarily as she turned.

A tall, blond man dressed in black trousers and a flowing red shirt was leaning against the frame of the French doors. His flamboyant clothes were in stark contrast to the staid navy blazers and khaki trousers the other men were wearing, and his expression was one of bemused interest. He looked young enough to be a graduate assistant. "Are you okay?"

"Yeah," she laughed, a little unsteadily. "I'm fine."

"Sorry if I startled you. My father told me you were here—I wanted to say hello." He gave her a crooked grin and stuck out his hand.

"Your father?"

"I'm Alistair Proser. Your new boss is my dad." He made a deprecating little face. "Not that you should be intimidated or anything."

For a minute, Katie paused. Alistair Proser was a name she knew she recognized, but the exact recollection eluded her. "I'm very glad to meet you." She shook his hand as she silently searched her memory.

"I wanted to say hello," he continued. "Especially since our areas are so closely aligned."

"Oh?" Even as she said it, the memory burst into her awareness. "You can't be—you aren't the Alistair Proser who published the book last year on Irish politics and the Catholic Church?'' She stared up at him. Alistair Proser was one of the most well-respected names in her field. His book on Ireland in the nineteenth and early twentieth centuries had been well received by critics and academics on both sides of the Atlantic Ocean, but she had never connected the name of the English Department chair with him.

He glanced down and shrugged, a sheepish little grin at the corners of his mouth. ''Well, yes. I am.''

She stared. He was so young—surely he couldn't be much older than she was. She felt completely intimidated. ''I—I had no idea. I thought you were at Yale—I never imagined you would be here . . .'' She heard herself babbling and shut her mouth to stop the nervous flow of words.

He gave her another boyish grin. ''Well, I was. But since I decided to apply for the Sean Seamus Clancy Award, I thought I'd come here for a semester or two, and concentrate. Although I have to say—meeting you makes the thought of spending long hours in a library with my nose in dusty old books less than appealing.''

She coughed a little. His attempt at gallantry was cute in a clumsy sort of way. But the thought that he intended to apply for the Clancy made her heart sink. There was no way she could hope to compete with a scholar of his reputation. She shook her head as if to clear it. ''I'm—I'm very honored to meet you. I'm just a little surprised—I never imagined Dr. Proser was your father.''

''Oh, please. Call him Reg. Everyone does.''

Well, she thought, maybe everyone *else* does. Somehow the thought of addressing Alistair's stuffed-shirt father as ''Reg'' seemed as incongruous as addressing her twin sister Meg as "Margaret." Instead she only smiled and nodded, and hoped he would think her as casually at ease as he seemed to be. "It's a very great pleasure to meet you," she said awkwardly, and berated herself inwardly for sounding like the most obsequious of graduate students.

"I think the greater pleasure is mine," he replied. He grinned down at her, and the wind suddenly ruffled his long, blond hair. He pushed a strand behind one ear. "I'm looking forward to seeing more of you."

"Well, well, Alistair." An older woman stood just outside the French doors. She wore a pink sundress, and her gray hair was twisted into a knot at the top of her head. "Home again for a visit?"

"Ah, Florence." Alistair turned at the sound of his name. The woman advanced, and he bent down and pecked awkwardly at her cheek. "Do you know the newest member of the English department? Katherine Coyle?"

The woman looked at Katie with a measuring eye. "How do you do, Katherine Coyle? I'm Florence Clatterbuck. I teach modern European history." She shook Katie's hand firmly and turned back to Alistair as Katie murmured an appropriate response. "I read your latest."

He seemed to stand a few inches taller and squared his shoulders. "That was nice of you, Flo. What did you think?"

Florence Clatterbuck cocked her head and frowned. "Your premise was, as usual, surprising and calculatedly controversial. However, where did you find some of your source material? I'd no idea some of those documents existed."

"Well." He shoved his hands into his pockets and

looked away, over the woman's head. "You know, sometimes you just get lucky."

Florence glanced at Katie, then back at Alistair. Katie thought that a troubled expression flitted across the woman's plain, square-featured face. "Well, yes," she said after a pause. "Sometimes you do." She looked at Katie and smiled. "It's been a pleasure to meet you, Katherine Coyle. I'm sure we'll be seeing each other once the semester starts. Good luck here at East Bay. And you behave yourself, Alistair." With a little nod, she marched back inside.

"So many new faces," said Katie. "I hope I can keep them all straight."

"Oh, Flo would never hold it against you if you forgot her name. She's a harmless old biddy who's been here forever. Coming back here is like stepping into a time warp for me. Nothing ever changes, as you'll find out." He stuck out his hand once again. "I should get back to work. I just wanted to make sure I said hello. I'm sure we'll see each other around."

"I'm sure we will."

"I'm counting on it," he said with a wink.

Katie watched him make his way through the crowd, laughing, shaking hands, and clapping other men on the shoulder. Against the drab navies and khakis, Alistair stood out like a golden child. He clearly was the fair-haired boy. She felt a twinge of envy. Some day—some day soon—she'd win for herself the same ease, that same feeling of belonging. Academia was like a club, a club in which one had to earn the respect of one's peers in order to be fully accepted. That acceptance and accompanying respect were only earned with hard work. She glanced up. The sun was just hovering over the tops of the trees. It was getting late. Inside, the crowd had thinned out. She would find Dr. Callahan—Terry—and say her good-byes. There was still so much work to be done at Pond House.

Derry eased across the floor, dust motes swirling in his wake. The little house was cozy now that she'd begun to unpack her things. He stopped before the sink. A white mug rested upside down on the drying rack. He picked it up and examined it. "Katherine" was written on it in a flowing black script. On the other side, a short paragraph explained a brief history of the name. So her name was Katherine.

Still carrying the mug, he walked into the living room. Books were piled everywhere. He reached for the closest one. The title nearly made him drop the mug. *Wolfe Tone and the Boys of '98.* Wolfe Tone? This woman knew about Wolfe Tone and the Rebellion of 1798? He placed the mug down, and carefully read the titles of the other books. Nearly all of them dealt with some period of Irish history. A burst of energy swept through him. A stack of papers fell to the floor and scattered, but he ignored them. Not only did this woman remind him of Annie so fiercely he felt as though he'd been pierced to the heart, but she cared about Ireland? And its history? A thought, which both amused and saddened him, crossed his mind: If Annie had ever been able to read a book, surely one of these would be just what she would have chosen. If only he'd had the time to teach her to read.

His ghostly fingers danced lightly over the books. The entire history of Ireland was represented in the titles, as well as the art, the literature and the religion. This couldn't be just coincidence, he thought. There must be some meaning to Katherine's presence, and her amazing resemblance to Annie. There had to be some reason for her arrival. Perhaps they were meant to be together. Perhaps she had the power to set him free, although the thought of leaving Pond House was less than appealing as long as she was here. He desperately wanted to talk to her—to find out who she was and why she'd come here and what it might mean to him, and to her. He'd have to try and see if there was some way to get through to her—to get her attention without frightening her so badly, she'd never want anything to do with him. The lights of a car glinted momentarily through the window. She was home. He'd stay for a while, silent and invisible, and try to decide what the best way to reach out to her might be.

Chapter Four

The sun had sunk behind the trees by the time Katie pulled her car into the open space behind the house. She fumbled in her purse for a moment, searching for the key, and prayed that the lock wouldn't be quite as sticky as it had been for Josh.

It was now or never, she thought as she got out of the car. When she'd left the house for the first time yesterday to take Josh back to campus, she'd left the door open. There hadn't been anything of value inside at the time. Now, with most of her possessions still in boxes, Katie thought it only prudent to lock the doors. But the last thing she needed after her busy day was trouble getting into the house.

She inserted the key and turned it, expecting it to stick. To her surprise, it turned easily, and the door swung open with minimal effort. She placed her purse on the couch and smiled. So much for Josh's dire predictions that she wouldn't be able to get back in.

She stood at the window for a moment, watching the waterfall. The white cat was back, still curled up on the footbridge, sound asleep once again. Piles of boxes rose around her haphazardly. She had to finish unpacking and start organizing her books as soon as possible. The semester would be starting before she knew it, and she had to get her syllabus to Fran Garibaldi by the end of the week. There were some things she needed to check before she wrote it, and at the moment, she didn't quite remember where those materials might be. She had to get organized to teach, so that she could continue her work on the article she'd hoped would win her the Clancy grant. It was on the sixteenth-century settlement of Ireland under Elizabeth I. It was a little ambitious, but she had thought she'd enjoy the challenge. Now she wasn't so sure. Alistair Proser's work was certain to make her own seem like that of a rank amateur.

She leaned her head against the cool glass, closed her eyes and let the sounds and the scents of the summer night wash over her. The insects sang steadily, and every once in a while a bullfrog bellowed. The air was sweet with the earthy tang of sun-warmed lavender and oregano.

Well, Katie thought, all she could do was her best. She would concentrate on doing a good job. Maybe the faculty at East Bay wasn't the warmest group of people she'd ever met, but with the exception of Reginald Proser, they hadn't been overtly hostile, either. A warning ran through her mind, unbidden. *It isn't the enemies of whom we know we must watch out for, it's of the ones we don't know we must be wary.* This was accompanied by a surge of emotion, a bizarre combination of frustration and longing, so strong that Katie frowned, puzzled.

Where had that thought come from? And why did she suddenly feel as if she was no longer alone, as if some-one else had come into the room? A chill ran up her spine and the hair on the back of her neck rose. That feeling of being watched was back.

She turned back to face the boxes, half expecting to see someone standing among them. But of course, there was no one there. *You've got to cut this out, Katie,* she scolded herself. You have to concentrate and stop day-dreaming. There's too much work to be done before the semester begins.

The telephone's sudden ring rescued her from her daydreams. She fumbled between the boxes, searching for the cordless unit, until she remembered she'd left it in the kitchen. She grabbed it on the eighth ring. "Hello?"

"I knew you wouldn't be able to find the phone." Her sister's voice was as clear as if she were on the other side of the room, not across the ocean. "How's the new place?"

"Meg?" Katie's eyes filled with unexpected tears as a sudden wave of homesickness and loneliness washed over her. She blinked away the tears impatiently. She was just a little stressed. There was no point in making Meg concerned.

"Of course it's me. How're you doing? How're the people? Did you dump Josh yet?"

"Dump Josh? What makes you think that?"

"He called me."

"Called you?" Even three thousand miles away, Ka-tie knew her shock was palpable.

"Yeah. He called me, asking me to talk some sense

into you. I told him he was being a jerk. I hope you don't mind.''

''No,'' Katie shook her head and wandered into the living room, laughing in spite of herself. She curled up on the couch. ''I don't mind a bit. It's so good to hear your voice.''

''It's good to hear yours, too. Things are going okay, there?''

''Yes, of course.'' Katie glanced around the room. Despite the mess and the boxes, it felt like home. ''I love my place. The people seem okay, too. I'm going to be fine, here, Meggy. Really. Please don't call Mom and Dad and get them all stirred up, okay?''

''Who do you take me for? Josh?'' Meg laughed. ''Look, this is expensive and I'm not the one gainfully employed. You call me next time, okay?''

''Of course I will. I'll call you Saturday when the rates are cheaper, okay?''

''We'll catch up then. I just wanted to make sure you were okay. Okay?''

''Yeah. I love you, Meggy.''

''Love you, too, Katie-did.''

Katie replaced the receiver with a smile. Her twin's voice had really cheered her. And the nerve of Josh, calling Meg all the way in Dublin and making her worry. She stood up and paced to the window. She'd know soon enough if he'd called her parents. Meg was right. He was a jerk. What had she seen in him?

She glanced over her shoulder, and fleetingly thought she should unpack at least two or three more boxes before turning in. But the summer evening beckoned. Above the trees, the evening star shone steadily, and the sky was a wash of mauve and pink and violet. Surely it wouldn't hurt to take a walk. She'd been so busy all day she hadn't gone outside except to help the movers until it had been time to go to the reception.

She stepped through the front door once more, feeling as if she'd reentered some magical fairyland. There was such an enchanted quality about the place—it must have to do with the fact that it was so isolated, she mused. She had no idea where her nearest neighbors were. She'd have to make a point to find out, in the event she really did get snowed in. There was no way she'd be able to get up the driveway to the road unless it was plowed.

She strolled across the footbridge, watching a cloud of gnats swarming over the pond. The cat had vanished. Dragonflies darted along the banks, and on the opposite side of the pond, a huge splash marked a frog or turtle's passing. The water gurgled as it fell over the rocks.

She paused only momentarily, not wishing to attract the attention of the gnats. A path led down the side of the lower pond and disappeared beneath the trees. She glanced up at the sky. There was still plenty of light. Feeling adventurous, she started down it, following the curve of the pond, until the path diverged beneath the bending branches of a willow. It was like stepping through a green curtain, she thought as the leafy branches brushed against her face.

The path narrowed until it petered out altogether. Katie paused. In the falling twilight, it was difficult to see exactly how far she'd come. Then a crow cried out, a loud "caw, caw," and she started. Something caught her eye up ahead, something big and dark and bulky that didn't look like another tree. She pushed through the underbrush, sticker bushes pulling at the thin cotton fabric of her summer dress and scraping at her lower legs.

With a gasp, she stepped into a clearing. Before her, at least a dozen stones, each higher than a man, were arranged in a double ring. Katie blinked in disbelief. Standing Stones? Someone had raised Standing Stones in a clearing at Pond House.

She touched the nearest, hesitantly, half expecting to feel a jolt of energy. Don't be ridiculous, she scolded herself. You really have to stop getting so carried away with this place. The stone only felt slightly damp and cool in the falling dark, and she could smell the moss that grew up one side. She bent to have a closer look. There was something odd about the stone near the ground. It looked as if it had been cut all the way through and placed on some sort of base. She peered down, but the night was getting darker by the minute. Soon there wouldn't be enough light to find her way back to the cottage. She wished she'd thought to bring a flashlight, but a flashlight was something else she needed to put on her list.

She started back through the woods the way she'd come, thinking all the time of what she knew about Standing Stones. It wasn't much, she thought ruefully.

Groups of standing stones or large megaliths dating to the Neolithic or Bronze Age could be found around the world. The appearance of a set at Pond House wasn't completely unlikely, in retrospect. But no one knew what they were for, although there were plenty of theories, purporting that the stones had sacred, astronomical or burial purposes. Hmm, she thought as she approached the sandy path that led down to the beach, could this be a sacred ancient burial ground? Too bad she knew nothing about Native American Studies. She might be able to interpret some of the signs or symbols she thought she'd discerned on the stones in the twilight. She'd have to go back tomorrow and get a better look in the daylight.

As she crossed the sandy path, she was suddenly overwhelmed with a feeling that someone else had joined her on the path. She quickened her steps, but the feeling persisted. She glanced over her shoulder. There was nothing. Just nerves, she told herself. Just nerves. Then the branches of shrubs moved, as though something—or someone—was brushing past them, and in the shadowy light, she thought she saw a glimpse of something white. "Who's there?" she cried out.

The shrubs were still. Nothing moved.

Completely unnerved, Katie ran back to the house, her heart pounding. East Bay was a nice little place, but that wasn't to say bad things didn't happen here. Josh would probably tell her to move closer to town. But there wasn't anyplace else. Fran Garibaldi had said so that very afternoon. One of the reasons the university had purchased Pond House was the dearth of suitable housing in the area. As she gained the steps, she smelled the same unmistakable scent as she had the night before, but this time it was much more distinct. A memory clicked into place. It was the aftershave her grandfather used to wear—a scent she associated with old men and Sundays. It was the scent of bay rum.

She slammed the door shut and locked it, and turned to see that a stack of notes on her desk had scattered on the floor. What could possibly account for that, she wondered, as she stared around the living room, suddenly more frightened than ever. The day hadn't been breezy at all, and the night was just as still. The whole time she'd been outside, she'd felt barely a breeze. That's what had made the motion of the shrubbery just now so suspicious. Could someone have been in the house?

Now definitely frightened, she ran to her bedroom where she'd put her tiny jewelry box with her few heirloom pieces in the bottom drawer beneath her sweat clothes. But the bedroom was untouched. Everything was just the way she'd left it earlier that evening. The little jewelry box snuggled safely in its nest of blue and gray. She sank down on the bed, the beating of her heart subsiding. She was being silly. There weren't any burglars in East Bay. There weren't any burglars at Pond House. The house was set so far back from the road she doubted a passing vagrant would even notice its existence.

She was getting herself all worked up over nothing. The movers had knocked the papers over. A puff of wind had made the shrubs move, a seagull had been caught in the shrubs, and that accounted for the white blur. A random combination of scents had blended into something that smelled a little like aftershave. She'd have a cup of warm milk and then she'd go to bed. Everything would seem different in the morning.

She walked to the kitchen, where she'd left her favorite mug—the one with her name and its meaning— on the sink. "Katherine" meant "pure." She liked that. She got the milk from the refrigerator and poured it into a small saucepan, then stared in dismay. Her mug was gone.

It wasn't where she'd left it, and she did so very clearly remember washing it and rinsing it and leaving it by the side of the sink at a very deliberate angle to dry just before she'd left for the reception. It was the last thing she'd done before she walked out of the house.

She closed her eyes, counted to ten and opened them again. This was ridiculous. No one would break into a house and steal a mug.

She walked into the living room and paused, hands on her hips, looking around. The mug was in plain sight. It was sitting by the fireplace on top of a pile of books. Katie's jaw dropped. Was she going crazy?

Slowly, almost as if in a dream, she walked across the room and picked up the mug. It was clean. So she had washed it, just as she remembered. She looked from the mug to the books. The volume on top was one of her references for her survey class: *Wolfe Tone and the Boys of '98.* She shook her head. Maybe she was going crazy. Standing stones, unseen intruders, mugs that moved. She should have questioned Fran Garibaldi just a little more closely about the house's "history." Maybe that was the reason the house had been vacant since April. She remembered her teasing words to Josh just yesterday. Maybe it's the ghost, she'd said, so carelessly, with a laugh. She looked around. The house was silent, warm, and snug, and looked like the last place a ghost would choose to haunt. She shook her head and returned to the kitchen with a sigh, wishing she'd thought to bring a bottle of her father's Irish whiskey. Her mother used to scold her father for having what he called a "wee nip" before bed. But at the moment, a stiff shot didn't seem like such a bad thing.

Black and menacing, the Standing Stones rose from the forest floor, the tops shrouded in mist. Katie peered up anxiously, trying to remember whether or not they had really been that high the first time she had seen them. Nothing but mist and shadows moved within the depths of the gray-green silence, swirling along the periphery of Katie's vision. She reached out blindly, half afraid of what she might encounter, trying to feel her way through the fog.

And then she heard the voice. It was clear and distinct, much clearer than anything else in the shadowy, twilit landscape, and she paused, sensing the bulk of the stones rising all around her. The trees seemed to lean in upon each other, pressing close together as if for support or protection. No, she thought, not protection. Suddenly she was seized by a sense of menace, of danger, and she felt something press upon her lungs, forcing the air out of her body. She gasped, gulping in great draughts of oxygen, filling her lungs as though she were a drowning woman. . . .

"Help me—I need help. . . ."

The voice rose high and clear, cutting through the shadows all around her. It was an Englishman's voice, the consonants clearly articulated, the vowels long and liquid. Katie jerked her head in the direction of the sound.

"Help me!"

The voice called again, deep and insistent, demanding, rather than pleading.

Katie cocked her head. "I'm here—where are you?"

"Help me!" There was an imperious, angry tone to the voice, as though the speaker expected help and was more frustrated than frightened. Katie shivered.

"Where are you?" she called.

"I'm here—help!"

"I'm coming—I'm coming." Katie pushed through the brambles and the underbrush, the sticker bushes tearing at her clothes. She looked down and saw that

she was wearing her nightgown. What was she doing in the woods in the middle of the night, dressed only in her nightgown?

"Help me!"

Katie forced her way through the trees, branches snapping in her face, scraping her arms and legs. The path circled and twisted, leading deeper and deeper into the woods. She looked down at her feet. They were bare, and the path was rocky. Sharp shells dug into the soles of her feet, and she stumbled, as the voice cried again: "Help me! I'm over here, colleen."

"I can't find you," she called back. "I can't find you!"

Then she tripped across what felt like a log. She looked down. The shape at her feet was long and black. To her horror, it reached up with a skeletal arm, one white hand extended and splayed like a claw. Katie screamed, stumbled backwards and fell, down and down and down, into the swirling mist.

Chapter Five

Katie bolted upright. Sweat ran down her back and her nightgown clung to her body. Her heart was racing. She opened her eyes slowly, still half afraid that the awful presence might grab her. The room was shadowed, but through the windows she could see the faint glint of starlight on the pond and could hear the waterfall. Nothing moved outside, and in her bedroom all was quiet and peaceful.

She drew a deep breath. Such a vivid nightmare. *That's what comes of wandering around in the dark by yourself*, she thought. Your imagination is already working overtime. She slumped back against her pillows. But the voice had seemed so clear, so distinct. A man's voice—and an Englishman's voice, at that. English—or Irish, she wondered. He'd used the word "colleen," which means "girl" in the Irish language. And he'd been calling for help, though demanding was a better word. What a curious dream, she thought. It was one thing to dream of being lost in the woods, with the Standing Stones for added measure. But to dream of a voice that cried out for help, and sounded angry because she couldn't get there fast enough? Oh well, she told herself, dreams were curious things.

But now she was wide awake. She'd make a cup of tea and read for a while, she decided. She turned on her bedside light, pushed back the sheets and gasped. Her nightgown—long, white cotton trimmed with lace—was torn in several places. Almost as though she'd been running through the woods.

Derry moved restlessly through the trees. There had to be a way to get through to the woman—to Katherine. He'd thought to channel the restless energies of Pond House in order to reach out to her, but the dream she'd just had had been too frightening, too uncontrolled. Surely there had to be some way to harness the energy he felt swirling all around him and get through to her. He had to get her attention carefully or she'd never agree to speak to him, let alone help him discover what meaning or purpose there could be to his continued existence in this perpetual limbo. She'd think she was crazy, she'd deny the evidence of her own eyes—at least that's what he'd seen time and again when living humans were confronted by the supernatural. And even if he could somehow make her pay attention to him, it might take months or years before she'd listen to him rationally. There had to be another way.

He sank onto the ground, and leaned against a stone. A mosquito landed on his arm and he swatted the insect away, then paused. Within a hundred-foot-wide radius of the Stones, he had a body. A physical body, which seemed to be as corporeal to him as ever the one he'd had in life had been. Perhaps that was the answer. If he approached her within that circumference, he might be able to make her think he was alive. And then, without the necessary nuisance of having to explain that he was a ghost, he could talk to her, and try to find out if there was any way she could help. At the least, perhaps she could help him find out what had happened to Annie.

This won't be easy, he thought. Winter was coming, and very soon she'd stay within the cozy confines of Pond House. He had a few brief weeks to make her acquaintance, and try to discover if the remarkable coincidence of her appearance had any meaning for him. But there had to be, he told himself. There had to be. He could feel it—he smiled grimly in the darkness—in his bones.

When Katie finally fell asleep, it was close to dawn. The birds had already begun to sing, and the insects were still. A grayish light suffused the sky, but Katie left her bedside lamp burning. When she woke, it was after ten, and sunlight filled her bedroom with a yellow glow. She got out of bed gingerly. All right, she thought. Let's assess this. The nightgown was fragile. She could easily have torn it without knowing it. It could have come through the wash with several rips, and she might not have noticed. That had to be it. After all, the nightgown wasn't dirty. It wasn't full of pine needles or anything. Clearly she hadn't really been out in the woods. Once again, she was letting her imagination run away with her.

Enough, she said to herself. "It's time to get to work," she said out loud. She pulled her nightgown over her head, tossed it on the bed and strode into the bathroom, where she turned the taps on full force for her morning shower. Nothing had happened for which there wasn't a reasonable explanation. And nothing was going to happen, either, she said to herself. She stepped under the steaming spray, vowing to think about nothing but Ireland for the next six hours.

It was terribly hard to concentrate, knowing that the Standing Stones were out there in the woods. Maybe, she mused as she sipped a glass of iced tea and stared out the window, maybe the Stones weren't real. Maybe she had imagined the whole thing. "Oh, stop this," she said aloud. She checked her watch. It was after three o'clock. Except for a brief lunch break, she'd been working all day. She got up and stretched. Surely she deserved a little walk. Just a quick one, she told herself. Just enough to clear her head. And check for the Standing Stones. Just to see if they were really there.

She strolled across the footbridge. In the sunlight, the water was dark and murky. It was impossible to see the fish. She followed the same path she'd taken the previous evening. In the daylight, it was much easier to see how overgrown the path really was. She was lucky she hadn't tripped and broken her ankle. She paused as the path intersected with the one that led down to the beach, half expecting to hear the voice calling, or to see the brush move. But nothing happened, and she chided herself for being so overly imaginative.

She pushed through the thick undergrowth, and stepped at last into the clearing. The Stones rose just as she remembered them, but in the light they didn't seem quite so large or menacing. They were barely as tall as she was, made of thick slabs of granite, about the width and thickness of a man. They were arranged in two concentric rings. The bases were thick with weeds and vines twined around most of them.

Katie pushed aside some of the growth. The Stones seemed to have some sort of markings on them, and she peered closely, trying to decipher the script. With a start, she realized the script was Ogham, the curious stick alphabet that predated the earliest Irish writings by the Romanized Celtic monks. So far, no Rosetta Stone had ever been discovered, and no one knew what the stick shapes meant. She would have to come back with paper and pen and make notes. As she bent closer to explore the bases, for it was clear that the markings were not ancient and nowhere near as old as the bases on which they stood, she thought she heard a rustle in the bushes behind her.

Her blood froze and she glanced fearfully over first one shoulder and then the other. But she saw nothing, and with a sigh, she turned back to examine the stones once more. She stooped down, brushing away dirt and weeds. The stones had been mortared into place upon the bases. She paused, considering. That meant the stones had been put there afterwards. The bases seemed ancient, the weathered rock pitted and misshapen. There was no doubt that the bases had been in place for centuries. But the megaliths themselves confused her. The carvings on them had been done fairly recently, although there was no doubt that the language in which they were carved was an ancient one.

A twig snapped beneath her foot and she jumped. Her heart leapt and she closed her eyes, leaning against a stone. Her nerves were getting the better of her. She would have to stop being so jumpy or she'd never make it through the first week, let alone the first semester. And then she smelled it again—the distinctive odor of bay rum—and felt an overwhelming sensation that she was being watched. She took a deep breath and opened her eyes. "I know you're there," she called. "Why don't you stop playing these games and show yourself?"

There was a long pause, and then to Katie's surprise, the sound of the bushes parting came from behind her. "I'm terribly sorry," said a woman's voice as Katie swung around just in time to see a tall, blond woman emerge from the underbrush beneath the trees. "I didn't think anyone was close enough to hear me. I was just coming up the path from the beach—there's a shortcut, you know, out to the main road."

"N-no," stammered Katie. Her heart pounded so loudly she was sure the woman could hear it, too, and her palms were wet. Katie trembled all over. She didn't know whether to hug the woman for being so obviously real, or lambaste her for scaring her half to death. Katie crossed her arms and hoped the woman wouldn't notice how she shook.

"I'm so sorry," the woman repeated. "I did scare you—I am sorry."

"It's okay," said Katie. She hesitated for a split second. The woman's long, blond hair and pale, thin face gave her a ghostly aspect but she seemed human enough. "I'm Katie Coyle. I'm teaching at East Bay."

"So you're the new resident of Pond House, then?" said the woman. "I'm Mary Monahan. Have they warned you about me yet?"

Katie blinked. Mary wore a gauzy white tunic over flowing white trousers. They enhanced her otherworldly air, but she certainly didn't look dangerous in any way. "Warn me about you?" she said slowly. "Are you dangerous?"

At that Mary laughed, a tinkling little laugh that sounded like the peal of church bells. For a moment, she sounded no older than Katie, and Katie wondered just how old she really was. "Well, I'm not an ax murderer."

"How about an armed robber?" Katie wasn't sure she quite believed the conversation. The woman seemed all right, but Katie noticed that the woman hadn't said she *wasn't* dangerous.

"Oh no," replied Mary. "I'm afraid of guns."

"Well," said Katie, searching for something to say. "I suppose that's a good thing."

Mary cocked her head. "But I did startle you, and for that I'm terribly sorry. I see you've already found your way out here to these. Interesting, aren't they?"

Katie nodded. Mary advanced. She circled the stones, caressing the nearest with a hand draped in silver bracelets and rings. The sunlight sparkled on the metal. "Yes, they are. I've got a lot of questions, but I doubt I'll ever find the answers."

"What would you like to know?" asked Mary. "My grandfather raised them."

"He did?" Katie asked, startled once more by Mary's extraordinary claim. It lent the whole exchange a decidedly eerie air.

"Yes," Mary said, not looking at her. She was tracing the stick figures with the tip of one long fingernail, which Katie noticed was painted pale peach. "He had an even more interesting reputation than I do, you know."

Katie blinked again. There was something at once appealing and off-putting about this woman, with her long, pale hair and pale clothes—something ethereal and fey. "Well," said Katie slowly, trying to think of some way to respond to the woman. "What kind of reputation do you have?"

Mary gave that same soft, tinkling laugh. "I may as well tell you, before someone else does. I'm the town witch."

"Oh," said Katie, even more slowly than before, and thinking twice as rapidly. How on earth did one respond to such a claim politely? *"How nice"* didn't seem appropriate.

Mary laughed once more, and this time there was a throaty quality in her laugh. "Not really," she said. "But my family has a reputation." She broke off and sighed. "Sometimes I'm not sure why I ever came back." She gazed off into the distance, and Katie was struck by a profound sense of loneliness in the older woman's gaze. She realized that Mary was much older than she'd originally guessed. With her long, flowing blond hair and gauzy clothes, she looked like a throwback to 1968. Which, Katie realized with a start, she probably was. A shaft of late-afternoon sun fell across her face, revealing lines and creases that the shade had hidden before. Suddenly Mary looked closer to fifty than she did to forty.

"Where did you used to live?" asked Katie, more as an attempt to erase the look of sadness that had crossed Mary's face than a real request for information.

"Oh," she replied. "For a while I was in Boston, then New York, and then Baltimore. After that, I lived on the West Coast for about ten years. But I came back when my mother died. I missed New England. All those palm trees and balmy temperatures got on my nerves.'' She flashed a grin in Katie's direction, and suddenly Katie saw that there was much more to the woman's story. Suddenly she felt as though this were someone she'd like to get to know, someone without the kinds of pretensions universities bred in career academics. On impulse, she said, ''Would you like to come back to the house for a cup of tea?''

Mary looked startled, and then a slow smile, far more genuine than her laugh, spread over her face. ''Sure,'' she said. ''Why not?''

''I'd love to hear more about the history of this place,'' Katie said as the two women walked slowly down the path. ''Why did your grandfather raise the stones?''

''Well,'' said Mary, ''he was a bit of a crackpot, I guess you could say. Maybe even more than a bit. He had this idea that the Stones could be linked to a set of stones in Ireland. So he made copies and, well, he spent a lot of years trying to get them just so. From what I can gather, they are pretty exact duplicates of ones just outside of Dublin.''

''Hmm,'' said Katie. She concentrated on walking through the brush. ''But the bases on which the stones are placed look ancient. Where did he find those?''

''Oh, those were already there. That's what gave him the idea, you see. He was always intensely interested in power points, ley lines, that sort of thing. You know what I mean?''

Katie nodded slowly. According to some, ley lines were lines of power and energy that ran across and through the earth, intersecting at various points. The theory attempted to explain why so many ancient monuments seemed to be laid out on straight lines.

"So anyway," Mary was saying, "At first he hoped he could use the Stones as a sort of portal to go back and forth between here and Ireland. When that didn't work, he had other ideas. He kept experimenting until the day he died, and just about drove my grandmother crazy. She refused to keep the house after he died. That's when it was sold to East Bay."

"That's a long time ago," said Katie.

"Yes. Over thirty years ago, now. But the house was empty for a long time before it was sold. My grandfather was the only one who really enjoyed living here. This house has a long history of turning over one owner after another. In fact, I think the university has owned it longer than anyone else since the eighteenth century."

"But why," asked Katie, genuinely bewildered. "Pond House is beautiful."

"It is beautiful," Mary agreed. "But—" She broke off, clearly hesitant.

"Go on," said Katie. "I have to live here."

Mary glanced around. They had reached the edge of the lower pond, and the sunlight sparkled on the water. Dragonflies swooped over the surface, and the water bubbled contentedly at the base of the waterfall. She took a deep breath. "Look. I don't want to scare you or anything, or make you think I'm any stranger than you already must think I am. You seem very down-to-earth— not at all like some of those overeducated idiots at East Bay."

"If there's a story, I'd love to hear it," said Katie. She put her hand on the other woman's arm. "Come on inside. I'll make us some tea."

Together, the two women walked into the house. Mary hesitated noticeably as she stepped over the threshold. "Ah," she said with a sigh of relief. "The place likes you. That's a very good sign."

Katie turned. "It is?"

"Oh, yes. You have a very positive vibration. It's quite clear. The house likes that a lot."

"Ah," said Katie as she went into the kitchen, wondering what else to say. She wanted to hear the story very badly, but on the other hand, she wasn't sure she could believe anything Mary might have to say. There was definitely something different about the woman, definitely something that the good citizens of East Bay obviously found more than a little odd.

She busied herself getting mugs and spoons and a sugar bowl. When at last she set a mug of steaming tea in front of Mary, she said, "Now. Tell me. I won't laugh or anything."

"Ok," Mary said, stirring her tea calmly. "The place is haunted."

Katie gave Mary a sharp appraising look, but it was obvious from the way Mary had said it that she believed that what she was telling Katie was the truth. "Go on," said Katie. "Tell me more."

"Well, let me see. You haven't been here very long, but maybe you've noticed a cat who sleeps on the foot-bridge?" At Katie's nod, Mary went on. "That cat's a ghost. You can't get close to her—if you go out to pet her, by the time you've rounded the rhododendron bushes, she's disappeared. And there's a holly tree that used to stand in the far corner across from the upper pond—sometimes you still see it, although it was cut down years ago to make room for the other trees. And sometimes, when things are going to go especially well for you, just near the fireplace—where the original kitchen used to be, before the house was modernized in the twenties—you can still smell baking bread. Most often it's very early in the morning, but sometimes at other times, too. And other than that—well, you've been down to the beach, haven't you?'' When Katie nodded once more, Mary continued. ''Well, legend has it that one of the wrecks along the coast was the wreck of a pirate ship around the turn of the eighteenth century. The pirate captain was washed ashore, and crawled up the path that leads from the beach. He died there, calling for help.''

Katie felt the blood drain from her face. ''Help?'' she repeated.

Mary shot her a sharp glance. ''You've heard it, haven't you?''

Katie shrugged, shook her head and wondered why she felt so flustered. ''Well, no, not really—I mean—it's an owl, most likely, or some other bird—calling in the night. . . .''

Mary was looking at her with sympathy. ''It's not a bird. It's the ghost. My grandmother hated him, the way she hated everything about Pond House. He wasn't a very nice ghost when she was around. He'd play tricks on her all the time—throw stuff around, move things. She'd leave something in one spot, and it would turn up in another.'' She was watching Katie very closely.

Katie felt very cold. She wrapped her hands around her mug and pressed them tightly against the warm pottery. ''Oh, really?'' she said in a strained voice. ''Tell me more.''

''That's one of the reasons Pond House doesn't stay

lived-in very long. The other reason is that the house itself has an energy—a feel to it. You've felt it, too, I can see that you have. You know what I am talking about, don't you?''

Suddenly Katie wanted very much to be alone. It was all too unbelievable. Standing Stones. Crazy grandfathers who thought they could be used to travel back and forth to Ireland. Ghosts of dying pirates calling for help. Disappearing cats and holly bushes. Things that moved all by themselves. She brought her mug uncertainly to her lips. ''Would you care for more tea?''

Mary shook her head, her brown eyes soft with sympathy. ''I can see I've upset you. Listen, the place likes you. I can tell. The ghost hasn't ever harmed anyone. He's more of an annoyance. My grandfather had this idea of going back in time through the stones to try and find the pirate treasure.''

''Have you ever heard the ghost?''

Mary glanced down at the mug and smiled. ''Well,'' she said slowly. ''Maybe once or twice.'' She looked up into Katie's eyes. ''I'm terribly sorry. I didn't mean to upset you. Pond House is a special place, and you must be a special person if it likes you. It liked my grandfather—but not my grandmother. Granddad used to say it would run her out at the first chance as soon as he was dead. And you know what? He was right.'' She drained her mug and stood up. ''I've taken enough of your time. Thank you for the tea. I'm sure I'll see you around town. And I'm sorry I startled you out by the Stones. I won't use the path again.''

''No, no,'' Katie said. ''Please, by all means. Just whistle or something. The ghost doesn't whistle, does he?''

Mary grinned. "No. Not that I've ever heard." She glanced around at the peaceful sunlit room. "I think you'll be good for Pond House, Katie Coyle."

Katie said good-bye to the woman and tidied up the tea things. It would be almost funny if it weren't so accurate. The woman had virtually recounted a list of every strange event she'd experienced since her arrival. As she settled down with her books again, Mary's parting words echoed in her mind. She might be good for Pond House, but the real question was, would Pond House be good for her?

Chapter Six

Mary picked her way slowly through the bramble-covered path. She remembered how carefully her grandfather had tended the paths that ran through the woods—as carefully as he'd tended the immediate grounds around Pond House itself. She paused beside the Standing Stones, running her fingers lightly over the uneven surface of the nearest block.

"Hello, Mary."

She jumped in spite of herself and frowned in mock annoyance at the tall man who stepped from behind the opposite stone, his tattered white shirt billowing as he moved. "I asked you a long time ago not to do that."

"Not even a 'how are you,' after all this time?" Derry grinned, showing even white teeth and a dimple in his right cheek.

She relaxed. Damn the man, or the ghost. How could any human being—or former human being, for that matter—be so unbelievably beautiful? She smoothed her hands along the sides of her thighs. "Hello, my lord of Kilmartin. And how are you?"

He made an impatient little noise, and the smile faded for a moment. "So we're to be formal today, madam?" He bowed from the waist, an exaggerated court bow that was as mocking as it was polished. "And may I be so bold as to inquire into madam's health?"

She laughed a little. "Oh, that's enough, that's enough. How are you, Derry? It's been a long time."

"An age," he agreed, coming closer, and her heart beat faster.

This was the man who'd first seduced her when she was seventeen, the man from whom she'd fled East Bay. She wet her lips and stepped closer to the stone as though for strength.

"How are you, Mary?"

"I'm fine," she answered. "I've been having tea with the new occupant of Pond House. Have you met her?" She was puzzled by the look that darkened his face. "What's wrong? Don't you approve?"

To her surprise, he gave a harsh laugh, and turned away, shaking his head. "I've seen her."

"She's quite a nice person, I think. The house seems to like her, too. Why don't you?" Mary watched him closely. The fabric of his shirt stretched across his shoulders and the dark breeches clung to his hips. As always, his feet were bare.

"I didn't say I didn't like her."

"Well, what it is, then? You can't hide from me, Derry O'Riordan. I know you much too well."

He turned back to face her, hands on his hips. "Oh, you know more about me than anyone else, I'll grant you that. But that woman—" he broke off and stared into space. "I cannot quite believe my eyes."

"What is it?" She sank to the mossy ground, patting it with her hand. "Come on, we're old friends after all that's gone between us. Tell me."

He raised one eyebrow, hesitated, and then settled himself on the ground, folding his long frame against an opposite stone. "She's the image of Annie."

"Annie." Mary cocked her head, and an unexpected pang went through her. "The woman you lost?"

Derry stared into space and didn't answer. He seemed to be lost in his own thoughts. Finally he said, "Yes. You know what she meant to me—still means to me—even after two hundred years. And that woman—Katherine—"

"Katie Coyle. That's the name she uses."

He waved an impatient hand. "Whatever—whoever she is. Her face is nearly Annie's. I can never forget it."

Mary watched him closely. "And what it is you're thinking?"

Derry rose to his feet and paced restlessly around the perimeter of the inner ring of stones. "Don't you see? Surely you of all people—with all your talk of balance and energies and flow—surely you can see this cannot be an accident. Her coming here must mean something. She's even interested in Irish history—"

"She's a professor at East Bay. Irish history is what she teaches."

"And you think that's an accident?" He stopped in midstride and pinned her with his gaze.

Mary wrapped her arms around her folded legs and leaned her chin on her knees. "Well," she said slowly. "I suppose I see your point. What do you think it means?"

"I'm not sure," he replied. He looked down at the ground. "It could mean that after all these years, maybe there's a way for me to break away from the energy that's held me here. Maybe there's a way for me to find my way to Annie—or maybe it means that she is Annie and she's found her way to me, at last. But whatever it means, I must get closer to her. I must get to know her—must get to find a way to—"

"Meet her?" Mary squinted up at him through the long shaft of sunlight that suddenly fell across the circle of stones. It was getting late.

"Yes," he said. "And I want you to help me."

"How?"

"I want you to help me pretend to be alive."

Mary stared in shock. The sunlight seemed to glow, and the air within the Stones seemed to pulsate with latent energy. "Derry," she managed at last. "I know you're very real—I know the Stones enable you to manifest physically within a limited circumference. But—" She stopped and began again. "How on earth do you think you'll ever do that? How on earth can you even begin to believe that she'll—"

"Because at least it's a way to get through to her. I'll tell her the truth soon enough. But she can't be afraid of me—"

"You've already got her freaked out. Between Pond House itself and a few of your antics—what on earth were you thinking?"

He shrugged and gave her that boyish grin, which still had the effect of melting her heart. "I was curious, that's all."

Mary shook her head. "I can't begin to imagine . . . what if I do some reading? Let me look some things up—maybe there's a way to break out of this energy field and release you. . . ."

Faster than she would've thought possible, he was beside her, reaching for her hand, raising her up so that they stood very close, with less than a foot of space between them. She knew her heart beat faster, and her hands trembled. Damn the man. He wasn't even a man—damn the ghost. How could he still have this effect on her? And what had he been like in life, if even in death he could make her feel like this? She wasn't some untried girl of seventeen anymore. Hadn't she learned anything in thirty years?

"Mary." He said her name softly, with that same caressing lilt. "You know I'm so sorry—"

She held her hand up even as she felt her throat thicken and the tears prick her eyes. "Stop it. Don't say any more. What we did was more than thirty years ago now. There's been a lot of water over the dam, you know? I've changed, even if you haven't." She threw back her head and forced herself to smile up at him. "That's the trouble, you know. I've changed but you haven't."

He looked sad. "You're right." He tightened his grip on her hand. "Please, Mary, say you'll help me. I'll tell her the truth, as soon as I can, I swear to you. Maybe it won't even be necessary. Maybe there's something she knows—something she can tell me, and I'll find a way to be at rest. Mary, don't I deserve to move on, whatever that means for me?"

She dropped her eyes, unable to meet the force of his bright blue gaze. "All right, Derry. I'll help you. I don't like the idea of deception. But I agree you should be free of this place. And I'll do some checking myself. I might be able to discover a way to lift this field, or at least interrupt it long enough for you to move on to a higher plane. You've been trapped here long enough.'' *Even if I don't want you to go,* she finished silently.

He raised her hand slowly to his lips and pressed a kiss onto the back. ''Thank you, Mary. I wish I could say I'd find a way to repay you, but all I have to offer—'' He broke off and grinned.

She blinked back tears and shook her head, smiling in spite of herself. ''You're much too handsome for your own good, Derry me lad,'' she said. ''I hope the next time around you come back looking like a mere mortal.''

''So maybe I'll get to die in my bed?'' he asked.

''So you won't break so many hearts before you do,'' she replied. She gently drew her hand from his. ''I'll think about this. In the meantime, you behave, do you hear? No more tricks. Promise?''

He stepped back and made her an even more exaggerated bow. ''I am madam's most humble and obedient servant.''

''Sure you are,'' she said dryly. ''I'll bring you some clothes tomorrow, all right? You can't introduce yourself looking like a refugee from a costume ball. You'll make the rest of us eccentrics look sane.'' She brushed off the back of her tunic.

''I await madam's return with baited breath,'' he said as he stepped back behind the stones.

''Until tomorrow,'' she called. The odor of bay rum accompanied her all the way to the beach.

Sunlight filtered through the canopy of trees. Katie lay on her back in the middle of the stones, staring up at the leafy covering like green lace, the blue sky peeking through. The ground beneath her back was soft and springy, the moss thick as carpet and warm in the sun. The stones rose all around her, protectively. Within their circle, she felt safe, welcomed. Nothing bad could touch her. She turned on her side, into the arms of a man whose face was shadowy and indistinct. He had dark hair, though, dark hair that curled down the nape of his neck and spilled over his shoulders. His chest was bare and he slipped his hands up and under her shirt, kneading her breasts with smooth, callused fingertips. She arched against him, feeling as though she floated in a warm green sea, her body aching pleasantly with need. It had been so long, years and years at least, since she'd felt this urgency, this pleasure. She pressed her mouth onto his, and his tongue gently circled her lips, teasing and caressing. Moisture trickled down her thighs and she spread her legs, willing him to cover her with his body.

Desire sparked through every fiber of her body, running down every nerve from the base of her spine to the tips of her toes. She gasped as he suckled one nipple, pulling the pointed tip deep into his mouth. She drew him closer, cradling his body in the shallow bowl of her hips. He raised his head. She saw at once his eyes were blue—bluer than any sky she had ever imagined, deeper than the depths of the ocean. He held up his wrists, and she saw they were chained together, the skin raw and bleeding. He gazed down at her with blue, blue eyes, and spoke, his voice deep and distinct and familiar. "Help me," he said. "Please. Help me."

Katie bolted awake, her book tumbling from her chest to the floor beside the couch, landing in a splayed heap.

There was no mistaking that voice. It was the same one she'd heard the first night at Pond House, the same one she'd dreamed called out for her in the mist. As she stared around the room in dazed bewilderment, the now-familiar fragrance of bay rum settled around her like a cloak.

The shrill sound of the telephone's ring startled her. She stumbled off the couch, her limbs heavy and clumsy. "Hello?"

"Kate? It's Alistair Proser. How's the unpacking coming?"

"Oh . . ." Surprised to hear his voice, she automatically smoothed her unruly curls. "Fine, thanks. It's coming along—I nearly have myself all organized."

"Well, that's great. Do you suppose you have yourself organized enough to have dinner with me tomorrow night? There's a new place in town that advertises authentic French cuisine." He said the last in an exaggerated accent. "Would you care to try it with me?"

"Why, sure." She looked around the room. It didn't seem possible that someone of Alistair Proser's stature would actually want to have dinner with her, but why not? "I'd love to, actually."

"That's great, then. How about seven?"

"Seven's fine."

"I'd come out to pick you up but my car's on the fritz. Could I possibly ask you to meet me there?"

"Certainly. That's not a problem at all."

"Well, great, then. I'll see you tomorrow at seven at Chez Yvette."

They chatted a moment longer and Katie jotted down his garbled instructions. As she hung up, she realized she'd have to call the place itself tomorrow and get better ones. But it was just as well. It would give her an opportunity to get to know the town better. The few glimpses she'd had of it, it had seemed like a pleasant enough little place, especially in the summer. She was curious to know how many of the shops stayed open throughout the year.

She glanced down at the floor where her book had fallen. It lay in a heap beside the couch. She picked it up. This was no way to start a semester, she thought. How was she supposed to make the material interesting for her students if she couldn't even stay awake herself?

With a sigh, she picked up the book. No more reading on the couch, she decided. She placed the book on the battered coffee table, carefully marking her place. As she crossed the room to retrieve another notebook, she noticed that the scent of bay rum had completely dissipated.

Chapter Seven

Katie drove slowly down the narrow Main Street, peering right to left, carefully watching for landmarks. She'd already passed the post office on her left. The library—"flagpole in the front"—was just ahead, according to the hostess at the restaurant. Chez Yvette was across the street from the library, tucked into a little storefront. She checked the clock on the dash. She was early, but she was eager to explore the town. She'd park the car in the restaurant lot—the hostess had assured her there was parking behind the building—and walk down Main Street.

East Bay was one of those quaint New England seashore towns that had two primary industries: tourism and the university. Without both, it wouldn't merit much more than a dot on the map. In the summertime, the population swelled to nearly four times the size it was in the winter, and in the winter the college students ensured that the local restaurants and shops were able to stay afloat.

She caught sight of the brick library, an American flag waving proudly in the brisk breeze, its base surrounded by a hedge of pink-and-white-striped impatiens. She looked across the street. A peach-colored awning had the words "Chez Yvette" imprinted in dark green. Through the windows, she could dimly make out palm fronds.

"That's it," she said aloud. She turned the corner and parked in the tiny lot behind the building, narrowly escaping scraping the side of her car against that of another patron.

She strolled around to the front of the block and peered at her watch. Six thirty-five. She glanced up at the library. The doors were propped wide open. She looked right and left down the quiet street. A few pedestrians strolled along the sidewalks. It seemed like an ideal time to check out the library.

Inside the cool high-ceilinged structure, she paused in front of the desk. The librarian was nowhere to be seen. Katie read the sign posted on the front of the librarian's check-out station. The library was open until eight o'clock in the evening until the end of September. In the fall and winter, it closed at six.

She walked a little ways into the stacks, peering right and left at the high shelves full of books.

"May I help you?"

Katie jumped. She had to stop being so nervous, she thought immediately. She turned. "Hello. My name's Katie Coyle and I'm teaching at East Bay this year. I thought I'd stop in."

The librarian was a stocky white-haired woman who

eyed Katie suspiciously. Unconsciously Katie smoothed
the skirt of her flowered cotton dress. The librarian
looked down at her open-toed sandals with something
like disdain and then back up at Katie. Finally, she nodded with what seemed like approval. "A new face at
East Bay? About time—some of those old fossils have
been there since year one. I'm Daphne Hughes, and I
can say that, since I'm one of those old fossils." She
laughed, much more loudly than Katie would've expected, and the sound echoed through the open spaces
of the building. "Would you like a quick tour?"

"Sure!" said Katie, amused by the woman's assessing stare.

"Come along, then. I just have a few more books to
shelve." The woman beckoned. Katie followed her
broad back down the aisles. "This section is all alpha-
betized fiction. Our reference and nonfiction sections are
arranged according to the Library of Congress system,
just like the library at the college. You're familiar with
that, I assume?"

"Oh, yes," replied Katie, practically scampering to
keep up. For such a large woman, Daphne Hughes was
unexpectedly light on her feet.

They reached the bottom of a flight of worn steps.
With a little shake of her head, Daphne said, "Upstairs
are the archives. The town records go all the way back
to the seventeenth century. We don't let too many people
in to see them, but we have an arrangement with the
college. All the faculty have access. May I ask what you
will be teaching?"

"Irish Studies," answered Katie as she peered up the
staircase. "So you'd have all the information about the
history of the town up there?"

"Oh, yes." The pride in Daphne Hughes's voice was audible. "Several years ago, one of the archivists from the college came here and arranged all the records. He made sure they were stored properly, as well. It was a huge project, as you can imagine. Took months."

"So, you'd have information about Pond House up there? The original owners and all?"

"Pond House?" Daphne Hughes gave Katie a measuring look. "Of course. You must be living out there."

"Yes, I am. Do you know the place?"

"It's been years since I set foot on the property. But it's a very interesting piece of land, I must say that. Beautiful gardens and stonework. Old Ronan Monahan left quite a legacy. What are you specifically interested in?"

"Well," said Katie slowly. "I guess I'm not sure. I've always been interested in history—I guess I'd just like to know more."

"Of course." There was a short silence, as if Daphne was waiting for her to elaborate. When Katie said nothing more, Daphne went on: "Would you like to see the archives? It's quiet right now—just let me put the bell on the desk so I can hear if anyone comes looking for me."

She swished away on her rubber-soled shoes, still talking. "I only have two rules: clean hands, and you put everything back exactly the way you found it. Order is heaven's first rule, and you'd think tenured professors would've learned it by now. But some of them are worse than first graders. Dirtier hands, too."

Katie held up her hands, palms out. "I washed. I promise."

Daphne raised her brows and peered down her nose.

"Hmm. You'll do. Come along." She hoisted her pon-
derous bulk up the steps. "You wouldn't believe some
of the ones who come in here. And you surely wouldn't
believe the dirt they leave around the light switches. I'm
forever going up there with a rag and cleaner. Of course,
I send John Sneed up there all the time, too—he's the
janitor; you'll see him around—but he's only one man
and how much can he do?"

What a character, thought Katie. Surreptitiously she
wiped her fingers on the back of her skirt, just to make
sure.

At the top of the steps, Daphne fumbled in her pocket
and pulled out a large ring of variously sized keys.
"Here we are!" She inserted the key into the door and
pushed, flicking on a light switch as the door swung
open into the room. She stood aside to let Katie in.

Glass-fronted barrister's shelves were arranged along
one wall, with black metal filing cabinets along the other
three. Two long tables with six chairs each stood in the
middle of the long, narrow room. Late-afternoon light
streamed through the tall windows opposite the door.
The room was cool and immaculately clean.

"This is the catalog." Daphne motioned to a large
ledger in the middle of one of the tables. "It's arranged
so you look up the topic you want—in your case, it
would be property records—and then the address. It will
give you a list of all the records of that property, and
where they are kept."

"Everything's here?" Katie looked around. The room
was fairly large, but the town was old.

"The oldest records are kept at the historical society,
and some are at the courthouse. We have most of the

more modern ones on microfiche. But yes, we have a fair number here.''

''Are you a native of East Bay, Mrs. Hughes?''

''Call me Daphne—everyone does. And yes, I was born here.''

''Did you know Mr. Monahan?''

Daphne rolled her eyes. ''Everyone knew old Ronan.'' She shook her head. ''He certainly had some crazy ideas, let me tell you. He was harmless enough. I used to cringe whenever I saw him coming. I was only the assistant librarian back then, and so I couldn't say too much. He'd ask for some of the most peculiar titles—I was always calling Boston, and there were quite a few I had to send away to New York to find. And his hands were always filthy—nails all crusted with dirt. Made me weep just thinking about it, I tell you.''

Daphne looked Katie up and down, and once more Katie thought she might demand to see her hands. ''You've heard the story?'' Daphne asked instead.

''Which one?''

''The ghost, of course. Pirate captain washed ashore and died on the beach.''

''Are there any records confirming the story?'' Katie tried to sound as casual as she could.

For a moment, Daphne looked taken aback. ''Well, come to think of it, not that I know of. It happened hundreds of years ago—there haven't been pirates along this coast since the middle of the eighteenth century. There are lists of shipwrecks, but those records begin after the Revolution.''

Katie was tempted to ask more, but glanced at her watch. It was already after seven. Any later and she'd be more than fashionably late—she'd be rude. ''This has been very kind of you. But I should be going—I'm meeting a friend for dinner across the street.''

''At Chez Yvette? The food's great, but watch your pocketbook. They cater to the tourists there.'' Daphne turned off the light and shut the door firmly. ''Just let me know when you want to see the records. Come any time.''

With a smile and a wave of thanks, Katie crossed the nearly deserted street and pushed open the door of the restaurant. As she stepped inside, she heard the muted clatter of cutlery and the soft hum of conversation. Despite the quiet streets, the place was actually crowded.

A dark-haired hostess who looked no older than sixteen approached. ''Hello. Do you have a reservation?''

''I'm not sure,'' said Katie. ''I'm meeting a friend—''

''Oh, yes. Dr. Proser. This way, please.'' The girl turned on her heel.

Katie followed the girl past tables clustered with patrons. The food smelled wonderful. She hastened after the hostess, who led her through the main room into a small alcove where Alistair was waiting. He rose when he saw her approach. This time he was wearing a rumpled navy blazer and khakis and a bright yellow polo shirt. His blond hair was pulled back in a smooth ponytail, and Katie noticed he wore a tiny gold stud in his left ear. ''You found your way here,'' he said by way of greeting.

''Yes, with no trouble at all,'' Katie replied. She nodded her thanks to the hostess, who handed her a menu as she took her seat. ''I'm sorry if I'm late. I was checking out the town library. Daphne Hughes is quite a character.''

''Mrs. Hughes?'' Alistair rolled his eyes. ''She's

something, all right. She was there when I was a kid. Did she give you her 'order is heaven's first rule' speech?''

"Yes," Katie said. "And I got the 'cleanliness is next to godliness' speech when I inquired about looking at the archived town records.''

"East Bay's records?" He cocked his head. "What on earth for?''

Katie shrugged. "I'd like to know more about the town in general. And Pond House has quite a reputation. Everyone I've met wants to tell me about it.''

Alistair shrugged. "Ghost stories. If you ask me, half of everything I've ever heard can be explained by the wind. The other half is overactive imaginations. When I was a kid, we used to dare each other to go out there. Scared ourselves half silly. It's a wonder someone didn't get hurt on that path going down to the beach.''

Katie leaned forward. "But weren't you ever the least bit curious about the stones? I mean, they look practically authentic.''

Alistair shrugged again and waved one hand dismissively. "But 'practically' is a far cry from *truly* authentic, you know.'' He smiled and opened his menu. "Hmm. I wonder if the marsala is any good here?''

Katie hesitated. She was about to respond that if old Mr. Monahan had copied the Irish set of stones faithfully, it might be worth studying the Ogham characters. Instead, she bent her head and opened her menu. They chatted about inconsequential things while the waitress took their order.

"So are you all ready for your first day of class?'' Alistair asked as the waitress set their drinks before them.

Katie stirred her vodka and tonic, watching the lime wedge bob up and down. "Well." She looked up at him and smiled. "As ready as I'll ever be. I have my two hundred–level course all worked out. It's the sophomore survey course I find difficult. There's so much material, and you can only cover so much in one semester. And when you deal with first-semester sophomores, it's even harder to decide how much they can absorb."

Alistair nodded. "That's true. I've always avoided teaching lowerclassmen if I can. I'd rather spend my time doing research."

Katie shrugged. "I enjoy teaching. But I know you're right. Research is critical."

He leaned back and regarded her with a superior air. "Not so much research. Publication is key. For example, the Sean Seamus Clancy Award—I assume you're familiar with it?"

She leaned forward. There was something about his attitude that was beginning to annoy her. He was reminding her more and more of Josh, as well as everyone she'd ever met in academia who'd struck her as pompous and overbearing. This wasn't so much a conversation as a means of impressing her. "I'm applying for it."

"Oh, you are!" He shifted in his chair and laughed. "So I think I'm coming home to write my article in peace and instead I find a wolf in the fold." He raised his glass to her. "Well, to academic rivalry," he said, sipping. "May the better man—err, paper—win."

"To academic rivalry," she echoed, sipping her own drink. She leaned back in her chair and wondered how genuine his jovial attitude really was. There were a lot of cutthroat rivalries in academia, and many of them were downright vicious. The last thing she needed was to make an enemy of this man. "I'm sure I don't really have a chance at winning," she said to break the silence. "I think the experience alone is important, don't you agree?"

"Without a doubt. I was applying for my first grants and scholarships by the time I was a sophomore. My father thought I was absolutely wasting my time, but all those experiences taught me some very valuable lessons. It isn't so much winning in the beginning, it's the fact that you're willing to go for the goal that matters, I think."

Bull, thought Katie. Winning absolutely mattered. She could tell he was disturbed. "May I ask about your subject?"

"Oh, yes," he said, leaning forward, his hands clasped in a steeple before him. "It's a bit controversial."

"A follow-up to your last book?"

"Not exactly."

"Oh." Katie looked around, wondering how much longer the food would be. "What's it about, then?"

He seemed to swell. "Have you ever been intrigued by the mysteries one so often encounters in history?"

"You mean, like who killed the Princes in the Tower, and what really happened to Anastasia? Sure. Have you uncovered another?"

"Not exactly." He dabbed his lips with his napkin. "I've solved one."

"Oh?" Katie raised her eyebrows and looked at him with real interest. "What's the mystery?"

"Have you ever heard of the missing Earl?"

"Of course," Katie said. "The Earl of Kilmartin was

a well-known dandy-about-town in late eighteenth-century London. He returned to Ireland to claim his patrimony on the death of his father around 1795, and it's thought he got embroiled in the Rebellion of ninety-eight. He disappeared from history in 1799, although his brother, Timothy, was sentenced to exile in Australia. Neither of them were ever heard from again.''

''Very good.'' Alistair raised his glass. ''I see you do know your history.''

Katie managed a thin smile. ''Thanks.'' Had he forgotten that she had a Ph.D., too?

''However, I've found out what happened to our friend.''

''Really?'' Katie was interested in spite of herself. ''Tell me, please.''

''Well, as you probably have gathered, much of my inquiry over the years has concerned the activities of the Roman Catholic Church in Ireland and the influence that the Church as a whole has exercised over the people and the politics. As you know, my book looked at the period from 1870 through the Easter Rebellion of 1916. In the course of researching my book, however, I uncovered various other sources, heretofore unknown, which clearly indicate that it was the Earl himself who betrayed his brother to the British. He couldn't stay in Ireland, obviously, after his brother was arrested and convicted, so he went to the Continent, and spent the remainder of his life living in obscurity.''

Katie sipped her drink. He was looking at her with an arch expression, and she knew she was expected to say something. ''That's very interesting,'' she said at last. ''And you're sure you can prove it?''

He shrugged. ''You know academia. There're bound

to be naysayers. But I spent most of last year in Dublin going through some fairly obscure sources which most have overlooked.''

"My twin sister's in Dublin," said Katie.

"I was at Trinity," he said, without acknowledging her remark.

"So's Meg," said Katie. "Do you know Dr. McKnight? She's mentoring with him right now."

"Tim McKnight?" Alistair raised his eyebrows. "I should say so. He's a pompous old windbag who thinks he's the foremost authority on Yeats in the world."

"Meg speaks very highly of him."

Alistair leaned back in his chair, waving an airy hand. "I'm sure he does strike people that way until they really begin to question him. Then he goes on the defensive. But it's inconsequential, really. He'll be out in a few years."

Katie opened her mouth, then shut it. Was there any point in arguing with him? She smiled politely as the waitress set a plate in front of her. She picked up her fork, vowing to finish as quickly as possible then plead a headache. The promise of the solitude of Pond House loomed like the proverbial balm of Gilead. Especially when Alistair began holding forth on his personal interpretation of Yeats. Now if only she could refrain from throwing her plate at him.

A full moon reflected on the pond as she drove her car down the graveled drive and the chirp of insects filled the night with a high pulsing chorus. She had one more day before classes began, and she wanted to put it to the best use she could. *Time for bed, Katie-did,* she thought as she got out of the car, grabbing for her purse. She stood by the car a moment, bathing in the moonlight. The trees were washed in a silver light that edged each leaf in silver gilt. There was no breeze, and she fancied she smelled the salty tang of the ocean.

Her evening with Alistair Proser—she hated even the thought that it could be called a "date"—had left her even more determined to win the Clancy grant. She would show the world in general, and the faculty at East Bay in particular, that she was as much the scholar as Reginald Proser's fair-haired boy.

On the other hand, she thought as she walked slowly toward the house, there was no reason to antagonize him. He'd treated her with that grating condescension so common in academia. Well, let him think she wasn't much of a threat. He hadn't even had the courtesy to ask her about her topic. Not that she would have been eager to share it with him. He probably would have sneered the same way he did when she mentioned Meg and her Irish mentor.

She felt a soft motion in the air beside her, almost as though someone had stepped close to her, and she told herself it was only a breeze. She inhaled, and was not surprised to smell bay rum. "You smell good, Captain," she said aloud. Maybe if she treated it like a joke, she'd see that the episode could be explained by the breeze.

But what about that mug, a little voice said. *You know you didn't leave it on that book.*

Hush, she told herself. With a sigh, she turned the key in the lock and pushed open her front door.

The room was filled with moonlight and the ghostly glow of her computer screen from the kitchen. She put her purse on the couch and flicked on the light. She looked around the room with a satisfied air. She'd accomplished a lot in a few days. The imitation leather was covered for the most part by a colorful patchwork quilt, and her bookshelves were full of her much-used books. Her trinkets, amassed throughout the years, were arranged on the mantel, the coffee table and the windowsills. The place felt like home.

She walked into the kitchen, intending to warm milk, but she was so full from the meal, the idea had no appeal. Maybe a walk would help her feel less like an overstuffed bird. She reached on top of the refrigerator for her flashlight. She wasn't about to go stumbling around in the dark.

Once outside, she flicked on the light. Its powerful beam illuminated a wide cone about fifty feet ahead. She strolled around the pond to the bridge, and crossed it. She glanced at the woods. It was too late to think about going into the forest, she decided. She'd visit the Stones again in the morning. For a few minutes she stood beside the lower pond, listening to the chorus of frogs and insects. She trained her beam of light on the water, and a loud splash made her jump. The water rippled in wide half circles. "That was one big frog," she said aloud.

"It was, indeed."

At the sound of the masculine voice, her heart leapt into her throat. Nearly dropping the flashlight, she turned to see a tall man standing beneath the oaks. "Who the hell are you?" she managed, wondering how fast she could get back to the house.

"Forgive me." His voice was deep and low in the evening quiet, and Katie was amazed to hear that he had more than a hint of a brogue. "I was coming up the path from the beach, and I saw your flashlight and the lights from the house. I didn't mean to disturb you."

"You didn't exactly disturb me," Katie said, noting with interest his finely chiseled features. She trained the beam of light in his direction and saw that his eyes were a bright and piercing blue, and that he wore navy-blue shorts and a white T-shirt. "Please don't sneak up on me."

"Forgive me," he said again. "I really didn't mean to frighten you."

"Who are you?"

"I'm—my name is Derry Riordan." He pronounced the name as "Reardon." "I'm visiting a friend of mine—Mary Monahan. She lives not far from here. You do know her, I think? She told me your name is Katie Coyle."

Katie eyed him warily. If it were true that he knew Mary, he was probably a bit odd, but safe enough. "I've met her," she answered. "Where are you from?"

"My home is—I'm from Ireland."

"I thought I heard that in your voice." There was something unsettling about the way he was looking at her—in the intensity with which he stared at her. "I teach Irish history."

"Mary mentioned that to me. She thought we might have a lot in common."

"She did?" Katie blinked.

Derry nodded. "She did indeed." He gave her a crooked smile and Katie noticed at once the dimple that appeared in his right cheek. He ducked his head. "I won't keep you any longer, Miss Coyle. It's getting late and Mary will be wondering where I've gotten myself to. Good night." He gave her a little nod and turned to go.

"Wait!" Katie cried. "What—what is it that you do? Do you teach, too?"

He hesitated. "Not exactly. But I do look forward to making more of your acquaintance, Katie Coyle." With another smile and a nod, he stepped back beneath the trees and disappeared from sight.

Katie stared after him. There was something at once compelling and disturbing about the appearance of the tall Irishman. He's too damn good-looking, she thought. Between the way he looks and the way he sounds, he'll have every female in East Bay swooning after him before long. She grinned, thinking that Mary was adding a new twist to her already infamous reputation.

"Katherine!" The voice echoed through the forest, deep and demanding and compelling, forcing her to follow the overgrown path. Her feet crunched over sticks and when she looked down, she saw her feet were bare. "Katherine!"

"I'm coming!" she called, pushing through the low-hanging branches that drooped in her face. The woods glowed with a bright white light that still wasn't sunlight, as though the trees were lit from within by some source of radiant energy that seemed to emanate from them.

"Katherine!"

She pushed through the last of the brambles and stepped into the clearing of the Standing Stones. He was sitting within the ring, leaning against the stone that was farthest from her. Warily she stepped between the stones, feeling the thick moss beneath her feet. "I'm here. What do you want?"

"Katherine." Derry Riordan's voice was deep and

rich and very Irish. With the peculiar clarity of dreams, she noticed that his clothes were torn in several places and that his feet were bare. He was also soaking wet, his dark hair plastered to his head. Drops of water rolled down his face and dripped off his clothes. He held out a pink rose, and she saw that his wrists were manacled together with a heavy chain. "Forgive me. I never meant to frighten you."

"Forgive you?" Almost without thinking, she reached for the rose. A thorn bit into her flesh, and she dropped it. "Ow!" She looked up at him. "It's real."

"And so am I," he answered, his face clear and distinct against the shadow of the rock. "And only you can help me."

Chapter Eight

No matter how hard she tried to concentrate, Katie found it impossible to get the images of that dream out of her mind. She found herself daydreaming several times, staring at the papers on the desk before her, and each time she shook herself. Tomorrow was the first day of classes, and she had so much to do to prepare. Including setting up her tiny office on the fifth floor of the Arts Building.

She was in the midst of placing her books on the rickety bookshelves when the telephone rang. The old black rotary phone looked as though it was one of the college's original telephones, and as Katie picked up the heavy receiver, she decided that that was exactly what it was. "Katherine Coyle."

"Katie?" The woman's voice was vaguely familiar. "It's Mary—Mary Monahan."

"Why, hello!" Instantly an image of Derry Riordan flashed into her mind. And Mary might be a bit strange,

91

but she was the closest thing to a new friend Katie had made in East Bay. "How are you?"

"I'm fine. How are you?"

"Oh, busy. Settling in. You know how it is."

"I was wondering if you'd like to meet me for lunch."

Katie smiled. "That would be very nice. Where shall I meet you?" As the two women made plans, Katie wondered how to bring up Derry. Finally, a bit too abruptly, she said: "I wanted to tell you I met your guest."

"My guest?" There was an odd silence on the other end of the phone.

How strange, thought Katie. "He told me he was your guest. Derry Riordan. From Ireland. Is that not true?" She tried to keep her voice even.

"Oh—Derry!" Mary sounded oddly relieved. "I—uh—I don't think of him as a guest. He's more like family."

"Oh," said Katie.

"You met him?"

"Yes, last night. I was out for a walk, and he was passing through the woods, and saw my flashlight. Half scared me out of my mind, but he seems very nice."

"Oh, that's an old habit of his. He's been scaring me like that ever since I was a g—" Abruptly Mary stopped. "Ever since I've known him. And yes, he is very nice. He's been wanting to meet you ever since I told him about you."

"Really?" There was something strange about this whole exchange that Katie couldn't quite define. "Well, why don't you tell me more about him at lunch?"

"That sounds great. I'll see you about noon, okay?"
With a click, Mary hung up.

Katie stared at the receiver. Mary was definitely an
interesting person—a bit odd, but friendly, and more
than a little lonely. She was obviously out of place in
this small New England town.

Katie replaced the phone on its cradle and looked out
the window. The window sill was thick with dust, and
she resolved to bring some cleaning things from home.

"All ready for tomorrow?" Alistair Proser stood leaning against the open door, arms crossed over his chest.

"Just about as ready as I'll ever be," Katie said.
"How about you?"

"Oh, I'm not teaching here." The tone in his voice
made it clear he thought East Bay was beneath him. "I'll
be working on my application, though. How's yours
coming along?"

She felt a small prick of guilt. "It's coming," she
replied. After all, he didn't need to know she'd barely
had time to look at her outline in the last week or so.

"It's tough when you have to juggle teaching and
all," he said. "How about joining me for lunch?"

"Oh," she said, silently thanking heaven that she
could legitimately say she had plans. "I'm meeting another friend for lunch already, I'm afraid. But another
time would be nice."

"Great," he said, straightening from the doorframe.
"It can be your treat."

"My pleasure," Katie managed.

"Alistair."

The stentorian voice made them both jump. Reginald
Proser peered around his son and glared at Katie with
undisguised disdain. "I've been looking for you."

"Well, so sorry, Reg." Alistair winked at Katie. "I was just chatting with Miss Coyle about her work. Did you know she's applying for the Clancy grant, too?"

"Is that so?" Proser peered at her over his horn-rimmed spectacles, then turned to look up at his taller son. "Your mother wants you to join us for lunch today. She's complaining that she never sees you."

Alistair shrugged. "Look, Pater, I've been busy. As a matter of fact—"

"As a matter of fact you found time to chat with Miss Coyle." The disapproval in the older man's tone was palpable.

Katie gathered her purse from her bottom drawer. "If you gentlemen will excuse me?" She squeezed past the two of them and made her escape. She had just reached the stairs when she heard Alistair call after her: "Remember our rain check."

She waved briefly and fled down the steps.

"My grandfather believed that the reason the stone circles are built on ley lines is that the Stones capture the energy somehow, rather like giant batteries." Mary paused long enough to take a sip of iced tea. She was watching Katie closely. "He also believed that you could direct this energy, harness it. And use it."

"But use it for what?" Katie asked.

"I'm not sure he was very clear on that point, myself. But I have my own theory."

"Oh?"

"I think the Stones do trap the energy. I think that explains the odd things that happen around Pond House. The images you see or smell or hear—the cat and the bread and the voice in the night—are all trapped in the flow. And I think that the ghost is similarly trapped there, too. He's stuck there somehow, and can't move on.''

''Move on?''

''To a higher plane. Earth energy is tremendously powerful, but extremely diffuse, so to speak. It's spread out over a wide area. But if the Stones serve the purpose I think they serve, they gather the energy and concentrate in one place.''

''That still doesn't explain what the energy could be used for,'' said Katie. She took a bite of her sandwich. The food was good, but she scarcely noticed it.

''Well,'' said Mary, ''that might explain how the ancients were able to build the things they did—the pyramids, and that sort of thing.'' She leaned back in her chair, and seemed to be watching Katie very closely.

Katie shook her head, and stared at her plate. Finally she looked up at Mary. ''So tell me about this visitor of yours. Who's Derry Riordan?''

Mary glanced up and around the room with a little laugh. ''Oh, if I could tell you that . . .'' Her voice trailed off. ''He's an old friend. He's really interested in Irish history. He has a special fascination for the Stones.''

''He said he wasn't teaching.''

''Oh, no. He's—uh—he's more into research at the moment.''

''Researching what? The Stones?''

''Yes,'' said Mary. ''That's it. That's why he's here. I hope you won't mind. You might see him around the Stones a lot. He won't bother you, though.''

Katie smiled mischievously. ''He seemed nice enough. And he's certainly easy on the eyes. As long as

I know he's a friend of yours, I won't mind at all.''

"Oh, Derry's a good person," said Mary. "He wouldn't harm a fly."

"I hope you understand. Living alone, out there at Pond House—well, usually I feel perfectly safe. But I guess old habits just die hard."

"I understand completely." Mary waved an airy hand. "Single women can never be too careful. But Derry's a gentleman."

"Hmm." Katie grinned. "That reminds me of what my father always said. Against a scoundrel he could teach me to defend myself. Against a gentleman he could only warn me."

Mary burst out laughing. "That's Derry all right."

"There is one thing that puzzles me." Katie leaned forward. "I had a dream last night that seemed so vivid, it could have been real. Derry was in it."

"Already?" Mary raised an eyebrow in mock mortification. "My word."

"No, no," Katie said. "Not like that. He was dressed in rags. And he was chained at the wrists. He gave me a rose and asked me to help him."

Mary blinked. An odd expression crossed her face, and Katie waited, wondering what the woman was thinking.

"Well," she said finally. "That certainly is odd." Mary looked thoughtful, but before she could speak, a shadow fell across the table.

"Well, Miss Coyle." The stentorian voice made her jump. "What a surprise to see you here."

Katie glanced up into the stony face of Reginald Proser. His thin wife, Lillian, was at his side. Her lips were pinched together as if she'd tasted something unpleasant.

"Dr. Proser, Mrs. Proser," she managed. "How—how nice to see you."

He folded his mouth into what could be construed as a smile. "And I assume you will be at the faculty meeting this afternoon, Miss Coyle? At two?"

"It's nice to see you again, too, Reg. And you, Lil," said Mary.

Proser fixed Mary with an icy stare. "Ms. Monahan."

"Hello, Mary," said Lillian Proser. She looked away deliberately, and Katie wondered what the two women had against each other.

"Of course I'll be there, Dr. Proser," she said. How could she have forgotten?

"I'll look forward to seeing you, then. Come along, Lillian." He took his wife's arm and the two of them marched off.

"Old goat," said Mary when the two were scarcely out of earshot.

Katie cocked her head. "You know those two?"

"Who wouldn't? He made a major pass for me when I was at East Bay. And I didn't let it die, either. I opened my mouth and raised holy hell, and his wife blamed me for the whole thing. I'm the one who left."

"That's dreadful," said Katie.

Mary shrugged. "It's happened to plenty. I'm sure it's not so different now."

"No," Katie shook her head. "Nothing's ever happened to me like that, but I know a few women who were . . ."

"Propositioned?" Mary waved her hand. "That's the past. But old Proser never forgave or forgot me, either, I can see that."

Katie looked at her watch. "He's not going to forgive

or forget me, either, if I don't get to that meeting. It slipped my mind completely. I'd better get going.'' She pulled some bills from her wallet and placed them on the table. ''I'm sorry to run out like this, but this should cover my share.''

''No problem,'' Mary said. ''It's all right, though, if I tell Derry that you don't mind his poking around the Stones?''

Katie got to her feet. ''Your grandfather put them there. Why would I mind if you don't?'' She turned to go and hesitated. ''Just one thing, though? Tell him not to sneak up on me. Last night he nearly scared me to death.''

Mary laughed. ''That's Derry. I'll tell him. I'm not sure it will do any good.''

The afternoon sun was warm on Katie's back and she glanced at her watch surreptitiously beneath the table, trying to stifle a yawn. It was already past four, and the dean of student affairs had been droning on for the last hour, describing the new academic standards for the coming year.

She stole glances at her colleagues. Most of them were listening with looks of polite interest. A few were openly bored, and one woman was obviously writing what looked like a grocery list in a small notebook. She looked up and winked at Katie.

Finally the dean sat down. Proser got to his feet. ''Well, then, ladies and gentlemen, I think that's it. Good luck with the new semester—my secretary will be in early all this week and the next to assist you with any problems, and don't forget the graduate students' reception tomorrow evening in Old Chapman.''

They all rose. Katie got to her feet, fighting the urge to stretch. She gathered her sweater and her purse, and as she walked past Proser, he looked up and pinned her with his steely gaze. "Miss Coyle. A word, if you please."

"Certainly, Dr. Proser."

He waited for the last person to leave. "I wanted to let you know that one of our graduate students was taken sick suddenly, and will be unable to teach her sections of freshman composition. As the newest member of our faculty, I'll expect you to take those sections. You can check with Fran for the time and room numbers."

Katie felt her lips freeze in a grotesque parody of a smile. Freshman composition? Another class to prepare for? "Dr. Proser," was all she could manage, "classes start tomorrow."

"Fran's still in her office. If you hurry, you can catch her. You can get a sample syllabus from her, too. Because this is a bit of short notice, I won't expect to see yours until next week."

Katie swallowed hard. "May I ask how many students that will be?"

"Fifteen in each section. We don't believe in over-crowding our courses. You can find the books you'll be using in the bookstore. Doubtless Fran has a few from other years lying around. Feel free, however, to choose your own, but make sure I approve your selections if you do." He smiled at her, a smile made all the more disturbing by its appearance of friendliness. "Any questions?"

"No." Katie straightened her shoulders. "I'll be able to put something together this evening. Good afternoon." She turned to leave, but his voice stopped her.

"And one more thing, Miss Coyle. Just a word to the wise. Mary Monahan is a troublemaker of the worst sort. No good can come of any association with her."

"Oh?" Katie kept her face as blank as possible.

"You're new here, Miss Coyle, and I don't expect you to understand. But I'm only warning you for your own good. Keep away from that woman. She won't do your future here at East Bay any good at all." With a brief nod, he walked briskly out of the room.

Katie stared after him. What an unpleasant little man. First he dumped thirty students on her without any warning, and then he tried to influence her choice of friends. The second made her far more furious than the first. She had half a mind to call Mary and invite her out for dinner. She started down the hall, still fuming.

"Well, well, what a pleasant surprise!" Alistair Proser's voice startled her.

She turned around, a careful smile fixed across her face. "Hello, Alistair."

"Here for the meeting?"

"Yes," Katie nodded. "It's just over now." She glanced down the hall, wondering how she could get away from him. She wanted to go back to the Stones while it was still daylight, and she needed to get to Fran before the woman left for the day.

"All ready for your first class tomorrow?"

"Absolutely. How's your research coming?"

"I'm thinking I might have to make a quick trip to Ireland in the next month. Too bad you can't come with me. I'll have to look up that twin sister."

Meg would just love that, thought Katie, imagining what her outspoken twin would say to Alistair and his pretensions. "Yes, too bad," was all she said.

"But I won't be gone long. Maybe only a few days. I just need to check some sources."

She smiled, saying nothing.

"So when can we have dinner again?"

"I'd love to have dinner," said Katie, thinking furiously. The last thing she needed was to antagonize both the father and the son. "But I really need to settle into my new schedule. How about in a week or two?" She hoped that was vague enough.

"Sounds great to me."

Katie glanced at her watch. "I'm terribly sorry but I have to run."

"I was hoping we could have coffee." He sounded a little petulant.

"That sounds great, Alistair, but I'm just overwhelmed today."

"I can see you are," he said. "Another time. I'll take another rain check," he added magnanimously.

"Thanks!" Katie hastened down the hall, escaping down the stairs. She fought an impulse to glance over her shoulder to see if he was following her. Her career at East Bay was looking less and less promising. Not only had she managed to make an enemy of Reginald Proser, she was going to have to find a way to dodge the attentions of his son.

She should put all the nonsense about the Standing Stones out of her head and get to work on her application, she thought as she got into her car. She should go home; make herself a nice, nourishing dinner; start organizing her freshman composition materials; and get to bed early. She should put all the supernatural rubbish behind her, and concentrate on the things that really mattered.

But she knew, as soon as she turned the key in the ignition, that before she did any of those things, she would see if Mary's "guest-who-was-practically-family" happened to be poking around the Stones.

Chapter Nine

Drifting beneath the trees, Derry sensed the subtle shift in the energy patterns surrounding Pond House, which told him Katie had returned. He coalesced within the circle of Standing Stones and reached for the clothing he'd carefully hidden beneath one of the trees. He had to remember to strip the modern clothes off his body before he disappeared into the vortex of energy, since he'd discovered, much to his chagrin, that the clothes simply disappeared, and that each time he manifested physically, he was once again wearing the same ragged breeches and torn white shirt he'd been wearing when he died. He shrugged on the unfamiliar shorts and shirt, fumbling with the zipper even as he felt Katie's presence coming closer. He had just managed to make himself presentable when she stepped out of the woods into the circle.

"Why, hello!" she said, a delicate flush on her high cheekbones.

He smiled in spite of himself. Since he'd met her the night before, the sense of connectedness to her had increased exponentially. He could feel the aura of energy that surrounded her pulsing with the vitality of her life force. She was so achingly alive. "Hello, Katie Coyle. And how are you?"

"I had lunch with Mary today," she said. "Did she tell you?"

He hesitated, thinking furiously. "She did mention something to that effect, I believe. Did you enjoy your lunch?"

"It was very nice. Have you been to the place? It's called the Tea Room." Katie broke off, cocked her head and grinned. "She assured me you weren't an ax murderer."

He raised his eyebrows, a little perplexed. "An ax murder—" There were so many things that his peculiar existence precluded him from knowing. "Ah, no," he finished lamely. "Not an ax murderer at all."

"And I told her I didn't mind if you were interested in examining the Stones. I find them quite fascinating myself." She moved to touch the nearest with a sweep of a graceful hand. "Tell me, what's your assessment of the Ogham writing? I think it's absolutely amazing that Ronan Monahan made such an effort to duplicate them, don't you?"

Derry blinked, thinking furiously. This woman wasn't just a replica of Annie. This woman was a scholar—she possessed more knowledge of Ireland and its history than he did, most likely. She'd know in a minute if he said anything wrong. He swallowed hard. "You're a scholar of Irish history, Mary was telling me?"

She looked up at him and smiled. "Oh, yes. And to

tell you the truth, the mystery of the earliest Irish alphabet has always fascinated me—even if I've never had the time or the money to really indulge myself.''

"What do you mean?" He moved just a little closer, and this time, he caught the barest trace of the perfume she wore—a blend of lilies and lilacs and honeysuckle.

Katie shrugged. "Irish Studies in America is just getting off the ground. Not every college or university has a place for it. In order to find a job, I had to make sure I could teach more mainstream topics—not something as esoteric and as specialized as Early Irish. Know what I mean?" She was tracing the stick shapes with one rounded nail.

"I can imagine," was all he could think to say.

"So tell me, Mr. Riordan, exactly what is your interest in the Stones? Mary said you'd be poking around here—you know, I may have some books at the house you might find interesting—"

"Doubtless," he interrupted. "But—uh—well, let's just say my interest is strictly amateur."

"Oh." She raised one eyebrow and paused, as though waiting for him to explain further.

"I . . . uh . . . I . . ." Derry cursed himself for sounding like a fool. "There's a set like these on my property in Ireland, you see . . ."

"Ah." Katie nodded, sparing him the trouble of saying anything more, and he sagged inwardly, thanking whatever power held him bound that at least he'd guessed the right thing to say. "You're the owner of the set these were created to duplicate? Where in Ireland are you from?"

"Well—uh—yes," he said, remembering the ancient ring that stood on a low, rounded hill on a corner of his ancestral property. At least two hundred years ago, they'd still been there, and according to old Ronan Monahan, they stood there still. "Yes. Mary's been telling me for years that these were here and looking so much like the ones I grew up around, and I—uh—well, I just had to come and see for myself. And I come from a small town outside Dublin called Kilmartin." At least he hoped to God it was still a small town. Old Ronan had said it was, but that was fifty years ago or more. Who knew how it had changed?

"Kilmartin." She said the word as if it meant something to her, then smiled. "So this is your first visit to America?" Katie turned to look up at him.

"Yes." He drew a deep breath. At least that he could say with certainty. "My first visit to this beautiful country." He indicated the forest around them with a gesture.

"It certainly is beautiful here." Katie smiled and held out her hand. "But I hope you don't intend to spend all your time hanging out in these woods. Mary must have some day trips planned, and such?"

"I—uh—I'm sure she does." He reached for her hand. Her warm, living flesh slid against his palm, and in that moment, he felt a jolt of energy, and a sense of a connection that nearly made him gasp aloud.

"I must be getting back to work, Mr. Riordan," she was saying. "It was very nice to see you again. I told Mary you should feel free to explore as much as you like. If you'd like those books, I can lend them to you. Just let me know." She gave his hand a little shake, and Derry was gratified to see a faint pink blush stain her cheeks. So perhaps she felt something, too.

"The pleasure was mine, Miss Coyle." He knew he

stared down at her, and he wrenched his eyes away from her face. He didn't want to frighten her.

"Oh," she said with a little smile, "Please call me Katie. Everyone—well, at least all my friends—do."

"Katie it is, then. And my name is Derry. To my friends."

With another smile that was almost shy, she tugged her hand out of his grasp, and disappeared beneath the trees.

Reeling, Katie nearly stumbled down the path. Who was Derry Riordan, and why was she so drawn to him? Yes, he was very good-looking, there was absolutely no doubt of that, but the intensity of her attraction to him transcended mere physical good looks. Why did she feel as though she should turn around and sit down within that circle of stones and talk to him as long as words would come?

And at the same time, he made her feel like a tongue-tied schoolgirl in the midst of her first crush. Every word of their conversation replayed itself in her mind. Ireland. Ogham. Kilmartin. As she crossed the bridge, she stopped short. Alistair Proser was researching the Earl of Kilmartin. The Missing Earl. No wonder the name had rung a bell.

The faint ring of the telephone brought Katie back to the present. She rushed across the lawn and into the house just in time to grab the phone as the answering machine began to play.

"Katie?"

Her sister's voice made her smile. "Meg? I'm here."

"So where've you been all day? Have classes started yet?"

"Tomorrow."

"Ah, good luck. I'm sure you'll do fine. They'll all love you."

"My students might. I'm not sure about anyone else."

"What are you talking about?"

Katie ran her fingers through her hair and sank into the sofa. "Oh . . ." In a few brief sentences, she outlined her run-ins with Reginald Proser and his son.

"They both sound delightful," Meg said when Katie finished. "And the son sounds like a real treat. How do you do it, Katie? You've gone from Josh the pompous toad lawyer to Alistair the pompous toad prof."

"Yeah, well," Katie laughed a little. "You know what they say. You have to kiss a lot of frogs before you find a prince. And speaking of that . . ." She hesitated. There was no point telling Meg about Derry. She didn't know enough about him to say whether he was a prince or a toad or an unemployed Irishman wandering the world.

"Oh?" Meg asked. "What are you *not* telling me? Or, more to the point, *who* are you not telling me about?"

"Oh, no one." Katie shrugged even though she knew her sister couldn't see the gesture. "But consider this forewarning. Alistair Proser is threatening to visit you when he comes to Ireland to finish up his research for the Clancy."

"What!" Meg shrieked in mock horror. "I don't need any more toads showing up on my doorstep."

"Well, he probably won't. It isn't as if you could help him. His topic is the Earl of Kilmartin. You know, the Missing Earl?"

"Mmm. Vaguely. Hey, listen, it's really really late

here, and I better run. But you take care, Katy-did. Keep all the toads on your side of the Atlantic, all right? And don't let any of them slime all over you—you'll do fine tomorrow.''

Grinning, Katie hung up. Meg always managed to make her smile. She'd have to ask Derry what he knew about the legend. It would be interesting to hear it from a native. She got up and walked over to the window. Outside, the early evening was calm and quiet and only the muted babble of the waterfall broke the hush. *Admit it, Katie,* she told herself. *It would be interesting to talk to him at all. About anything. It's just one of those feelings.*

A flash of white and a motion on the other side of the pond caught her eye, and she peered more closely outside. The flash of white came again. Someone was in the trees. She wondered if she should call the police. She pressed her face closer to the glass, and reached for the switch by the door labeled ''floodlights.'' Light washed over the lawn. She squinted hard, trying to see, but there was nothing. Just a bird or something. Or maybe Derry on his way back to Mary's house. Wherever that was. Funny, she hadn't yet asked.

She turned away from the window with a sigh, and settled herself with her notes on the couch. Time to put everything but class tomorrow out of her mind. She drew a deep breath and smelled the familiar odor of bay rum. *Now you behave, Captain,* she thought. As if in answer, she could have sworn she heard a soft chuckle.

It was much later when she heard the voice. Soft at first, no more than a whisper, it came just as she laid her book across her knees and raised her hands to rub her temples. She paused in midstroke and looked around.

It came again, stronger and more distinct: a man's voice, crying out for help.

She got to her feet and quickly opened the front door. She leaned outside and heard the voice once more.

"Help me! Help me!"

That's it, she thought. She ran into the kitchen and grabbed her flashlight. She was going to find out the source of that voice if it was the last thing she did. And if it happens to belong to some homicidal maniac, it just might be that, her conscience scolded.

Ignoring the voice of common sense, Katie dashed along the path, the strong beam of light bobbing before her.

"Help me!"

The voice echoed eerily through the forest. Heedless of the thornbushes that lined the path, Katie ran through the forest, her sandals slapping over the pine-covered earth. She reached the place where the path divided into the one that led to the road and the other, which led down to the beach. Except for the insects' shrill chorus, the night was silent.

She took a few steps toward the beach and heard the soft sigh of the ocean. Nothing. Doubtfully, she started down the path, training her flashlight first right then left. At the top of the little overhang, she stopped and gazed out over the dark waves. Ribbons of white foam laced the black water. The scent of the salt air filled her nose, and she breathed deeply, closing her eyes. She slowly exhaled and drew another deep breath. This time she was startled to detect another scent—a scent that was becoming all too familiar. Bay rum.

She jerked around and strained to hear above the ocean. The bushes parted and to her complete astonishment, Derry Riordan stepped out of the forest.

"Derry! What are you doing here?"

"Good evening, Kate." He paused just outside of the forest's perimeter and thrust his hands in his pockets. "I'm glad to see there's someone else who appreciates a moonlit ramble."

Katie laughed a little uncertainly. The odor of bay rum wafted by on the gentle breeze, and was replaced by the stronger smell of the sea. His words had struck an unexpected chord. "You know, I just thought of something. Something I hadn't thought of in years."

"Oh?" He stood his ground, although he rocked forward on his feet as though he'd like to come closer.

Her heart beat just a little faster. "When I was a little girl, everyone always called me Katie. Except for my grandfather. When I was a very little girl, he used to call me Kate. Sweet Kate, he'd say—just like sweet cake." She laughed again, very softly. "It's funny—I hadn't thought of that in . . . so long I can't remember."

"So you like to be reminded of forgotten things, do you, Katie Coyle?" His soft brogue added an unexpected caress to her name.

"Well, I suppose I must." She shoved her own hands into the pockets of her jeans and shivered a little. The ocean air cut through the thin cotton of her sweater. "But what on earth are you doing out here? And dressed just like that?" She gestured to his T-shirt and shorts. "Aren't you chilly?"

He shuffled his feet back and forth. "A bit. I don't really feel the cold, though."

"And why's that?" She lifted her chin and raised one eyebrow at him, expecting him to say something bantering.

Instead he shrugged as though uncomfortable and un-
sure of how to answer. "Just my nature, I guess." He
looked down at his bare feet and then quickly back at
her. "So tell me, Katie Coyle, are you just out for a
ramble in the moonlight?"

"No," she said, squaring her shoulders. She was going to tell the truth. If he knew Mary, he must know the
legend. "I thought I heard a voice. Calling for help."
She gave a little nod to emphasize her words, daring
him to challenge her.

"Ah," was all he said.

"You heard it, too?"

"I have, on occasion." He spoke slowly, as if choos-
ing his words carefully.

"And not tonight?"

"Uh—no. Not tonight."

"I heard it. So I grabbed my light and came out here.
I wanted to see once and for all—" Abruptly she broke
off. What was she going to say? *That I'm not crazy?*

"You aren't crazy," he said, and startled, she stared
up at him.

"Are you reading my mind?"

"Of course not." He sounded slightly offended. "Is
that what you were thinking?"

"Yeah," she said slowly. "I was." She looked
around. "Well, there's clearly no one here but us, so I
suppose—"

"The legend must be true?"

She gave another short laugh. "I imagine there've
been plenty of shipwrecks along these shores—look at
those rocks." He was staring out at the dark ocean. The
rocks glistened in the moonlight. "They're so beautiful
from here—"

"But deadly." His tone was terse. "I hate the sea."

The intensity in his voice confused her. "Hate it? I guess it is dangerous—"

"You've no idea how dangerous," he said. For a long moment he was silent, staring into the water. "A ship can be smashed to smithereens in a matter of moments against those rocks. And the poor wretches aboard her never have a chance," he finished bitterly.

"I haven't spent very much time sailing," said Katie, wondering why he sounded so vehement. "But I'm sure you're right." She paused briefly, and then asked, "So what are you doing out here?"

"Just walking." He gazed up at the stars. "It's a beautiful night."

"Yes," she said. "It is."

"I'm sorry. I didn't mean to sound so abrupt. It's just—just that I lost a great deal to the sea once, and I've never been able to forget it. Please forgive me."

"There's nothing to forgive." Katie had the feeling he wanted to tell her more, but his next words surprised her.

"I was—uh—I was wondering if you could perhaps tell me about a certain person in history."

"Oh?"

"The Earl of Kilmartin. He lived around 1799. . . ."

"Of course," she nodded. "The Missing Earl."

"I thought perhaps you being a scholar, you could tell me if you knew anything of him. Or of what happened to him."

"Oh, well," Katie drew a deep breath. "It's funny—I was wondering if there was anything about him you could tell me, since you're from that part of Ireland. He's missing, of course. I mean, he disappeared and no

one really knows what happened to him. It was never
very clear where he sided in the Rebellion of ninety-
eight—that's 1798, you know. . . .'' She heard herself
revert to her ''teacher voice'' and she inwardly groaned.
''Well, anyway, he had a brother who I believe was very
active in the rebel cause, but the earl himself remained
nonpartisan for a very long time. If he got embroiled at
all, it had to have been no earlier than 1796. But anyway,
it seems likely that he probably did, and either he or his
brother got arrested either late in ninety-eight or early in
ninety-nine, and most likely he died in prison. There
aren't any records of him, at least not anywhere I know
of.''

''Ah.'' Derry was gazing out over the ocean. The
wind ruffled his hair, and in the harsh light of the flashlight, his cheekbones were thrown in sharp relief.

''I'm sorry I can't tell you more, but—'' She stopped.
Did she dare mention Alistair Proser and his project?
Well, why not? If Derry found out some information
about his town, and Alistair thought perhaps she had a
possible beau and maybe would stop asking her out,
what was the harm? ''There's someone at East Bay who
might be able to tell you more.''

''Oh?'' Derry looked hopeful.

''His name is Alistair Proser and he's not on the faculty, but he's the son of the chairman of my department.
And he's here, on sabbatical from Yale. He's working
on a paper that involves the Earl of Kilmartin.''

''Is he, now?''

''Yes. He seems to believe he has the answer to the
mystery.''

She heard the swift intake of his breath. ''How so?''

''I—well, to tell you the truth, I haven't asked. But,

if you're interested, I'll get his phone number for you, and you can call if you like. I'm sure Alistair would love to discuss his pet theory. Most academics do, you know." She shuddered inwardly at the thought of asking Alistair for his phone number.

"Ah, well," Derry shuffled his feet. She could see goose bumps rising on his arms. "That's very kind of you, but—"

"It's no bother at all, really."

Derry raised his head and smiled at her, and once again she was unnerved by the thought that he somehow knew what she was thinking. "Well, now, I'll tell you what. Why don't you bring this professor friend right here? I can ask him myself." His blue eyes glinted in the light. She noticed how they crinkled at the corners when he smiled, and suddenly she felt as if they understood each other very well.

"That sounds like a plan," she said. She shivered a little as the wind blew harder across the beach. "It's getting colder and you don't have a jacket. I should let you go."

"I should let you go," he said. "Classes start tomorrow."

"Why, yes. How did you know?"

"Mary must have mentioned it."

She extended her hand, and he reached for it. His palm was cool and dry and smooth against her own, and a little tingle seemed to reverberate up her arm. "Good night, Derry."

"Good night, Katie Coyle."

"Will you be all right? You don't have a flashlight?"

"I'll be fine."

She hesitated, then turned away. At the edge of the

forest she turned back to wave good-bye, and stopped
short in disbelief. There was no sign of the man she'd
been talking to for the last fifteen or twenty minutes.
He'd disappeared as completely as if he were made of
smoke.

Water crashed over the chained men, frothing over the
splintering planks of the floor. The ship heaved and
shook. Wind roared. The lone lantern swung violently
from a hook in the ceiling, casting its eerie flicker over
the rows of prisoners. The men screamed and cried for
mercy, but Katie knew, with the curious detachment of
dreams, that there was no mercy, that anyone who
could've saved them was much too busy trying to save
themselves.

The sides of the hold creaked against the strain of the
wild sea, and the ship tilted and spun. Frantically, Katie
tried to do something, anything, to help the prisoners,
who screamed even louder, cursing and praying. But this
dream was one of those kind like a film, where all she
could do was watch and listen.

There was a tremendous crack, and the entire hold
broke apart. The sea rushed in, and a huge rock rose in
the center of what had been the hold. Men smashed
against it, whirling in the vortex of water, helpless as
rag dolls.

Katie felt the icy shock of the cold water, and she
struggled to breathe. She, too, was suddenly trapped in
the swirling tide, but suddenly another wave caught her
up in its relentless grip and threw her clear of the wreck-
age of the ship. She paddled frantically. The night was
dark, and she could barely make out the jagged outlines
of a rock as the water lifted her up. She hit the rock and

bounced away. Sand scraped her side, and she felt herself tossed as carelessly as a shell onto the beach.

An icy wind cut through her wet clothes and she shivered, gasping for breath. She tried to rise, but another wave knocked her flat. She breathed in a mouthful of water, and struggled once more to sit up, choking. "Help me," she managed to gasp. A dark shape loomed above her and she reached up, grasping desperately at what she hoped was a human hand. "Help me," she cried again as a warm hand closed around hers, the grip strong and sure. "Help me!"

"I'm here to help you, Katie Coyle," said Derry, his eyes bright in the moonlight, his tattered clothes dripping wet, his wrists manacled with a heavy chain.

It swung and glittered in the moonlight as he lifted her out of the water. "Why are you here, Derry?" she asked, as he cradled her close. Warmth emanated from his body to hers, and the waves receded to nothing more than a frothy swirl around his bare feet.

"To save you," he replied. "From something you were never meant to see."

Chapter Ten

"Alistair!" Katie stared in astonishment at the man who stood just outside the screen door. The morning sun glinted on his earring.

"I happened to be in the neighborhood," he said, grinning at her as though certain of his welcome. "Thought I'd stop by and say hello. Seemed to be the neighborly thing to do," he finished in a mock eastern Massachusetts drawl.

"That's so nice of you." Katie swallowed hard. She glanced over her shoulder. Books and papers were scattered all over the living room floor in carefully organized heaps. She'd worked long into the night on her paper.

"Aren't you going to ask me in?"

"Of course." She pushed open the screen door and stood aside to let him enter.

"Looks like a hurricane went through this place." He stopped just inside the door, glancing around.

"Well," she began, and then paused. What did she

care what he thought? "You know what academic organization is like." She beckoned. "Would you like some coffee?"

"Sure."

He followed her into the kitchen, carefully stepping over the heaps of books.

"Cream or sugar?"

"Nah." He cupped the mug in both hands and leaned against the table.

Katie poured herself a cup, more to occupy her hands than because she really wanted one.

"This really is quite a place," he said, gazing out the window.

"Would you like to see more? Come on." Katie was halfway across the living room before he had a chance to answer. "Let's take a walk."

"Oh, sure." He loped after her, setting the mug down on the windowsill as he followed her out the door. "How'd your first day of classes go yesterday?"

"Quite well." She followed the path around the upper pond.

"I knew you'd be home," he said. "I checked your schedule."

"Ah." She could think of no other polite way to respond. It really wasn't such an awful thing, she supposed. There was just something about him that rubbed her the wrong way. "Well, actually, I'm glad you did stop by."

"Oh?" He smiled into her eyes and inwardly she cringed.

"Yes, I was planning on dropping you a note or giving you a call. I've met someone who's very interested in your Clancy topic."

"Who?" The hostility in his voice made her pause in midstep and stare up at him.

"An Irishman, actually," Katie replied slowly, wondering why he was practically glaring at her. "He happens to come from Kilmartin. He was asking me what I knew about the Missing Earl and I told him as much as I could. But I figured you were the one he should really talk to, you know? And to think I was going to ask him what he knew about it."

Alistair turned and looked at her. "Just who is this fellow?"

"Just a friend," she replied. "Why?"

"Someone you know here?"

"He's here, but not at the university." She shot Alistair a quick look. He was staring at her with a furrow between his eyes. "Oh, no, he's not an academic, if that's what you're asking me. Not at all. Just someone who comes from Kilmartin and happens to be interested in his local history."

"And just how did you meet him?"

Katie ignored the querulous quality in Alistair's voice. "Poking around Pond House, actually. Well, not the house itself, you understand. In the woods. By that ring of stones—you know the ones I mean?" When Alistair nodded she continued. "It just so happens he owns the property where the originals are in Ireland."

"You don't say?" Alistair was leaning back. "I happen to know for a fact that that property—the estate of the Earl of Kilmartin, actually—was deeded to the Church of Ireland in 1805. It's never been sold."

A chill went down Katie's spine, and she glanced at Alistair, but before she had a chance to say anything, he pointed into the trees. "Is that someone over there in the woods?"

Katie squinted at the direction in which he was pointing. "Why, yes, I think that's Derry now." She smiled up at Alistair, all the time her mind racing. Had Derry deliberately misled her? Or had she simply misunderstood what he'd said? There was no reason or purpose she could think of for him to lie to her. "Let's go say hello, shall we?"

"Sure." His terse tone of voice was less than agreeable.

She broke through the trees, inexplicably happy that Derry had interrupted Alistair's visit. "I told him everything I know—which, believe me, isn't much. Anything past 1700 is a bit of a black hole to me, you know." She knew she was chattering, but she didn't care. Where in the world had Derry gotten to?

"Ah, Katie, where exactly are we going?" Alistair was picking his way through the underbrush, overhanging branches poking at his head.

"The Stones are just up ahead. I bet that's where we'll meet him. He's very interested in them." Seems to spend all his time there, she thought suddenly.

Abruptly the path ended in the clearing. Derry was squatting on his heels before the largest of the interior stones, making notes on a yellow pad of paper. He rose slowly to his feet when he saw Katie and Alistair. "Good morning." He spoke directly to Katie, his blue eyes meeting hers, and she felt her heart skip a beat. The feeling of being rescued from last night's dream returned, and for a moment, she wondered what it would feel like to rest her head in the hollow of his shoulder, to feel his arms around her, strong and warm and sure.

She lowered her eyes and hoped she hadn't blushed. "Hello, Derry. I—I hope we're not disturbing you at your research, but this is the person I was telling you about. He's writing a paper on the Missing Earl. He's much more of an expert than I'll ever be."

Derry's gaze slid from her face to Alistair's as a lazy grin spread across his face. "I wouldn't be so sure of that, Katie Coyle." He squared his shoulders and extended his hand toward Alistair. "A pleasure to make your acquaintance, sir. I'm Derry Riordan."

Alistair raised one eyebrow. The two men were clearly sizing one another up. "I'm Professor Proser. It's nice to meet you, too." The expression on his face said quite the opposite.

"I'm sorry to just barge in like this, Derry," Katie said to cover the awkward silence. "But Alistair came by unexpectedly, and I thought you two might appreciate the chance to meet."

"I appreciate your thinking of me." Derry's eyes met hers once more. "I'm actually more interested in the Kilmartin family," he said to Alistair. "Can you tell me what happened to the brother?"

"Oh, he was shipped off to Australia and was never heard from again," said Alistair with an airy wave. "And as for the Earl himself—well, he turned up on the Continent about ten years later. After having betrayed his brother to the English, he couldn't very well stay in Ireland. He fled to Germany with a price on his head, and lived quietly in exile until his death in 1854."

An odd expression darkened Derry's face. "Indeed?"

"Very similar story to Bonnie Prince Charlie. You know who he was, of course?"

"Of course," answered Derry. His blue eyes were

fixed on Alistair in an icy stare, and Katie almost shivered. "And may I ask you how you came to discover all this?"

"Well, unfortunately, you can't." Alistair spread his hands. "That's what I'll be discussing in my paper. The revelation of the identity and the resolution to the mystery will score me a minor coup in academic circles." He smiled unpleasantly. "I hope you understand I can't yet really speak of it."

"Of course not."

"But if you have any other questions, let me give you my telephone number. I'll be happy to talk to you at greater length another time, but I must be getting on my way."

"It was kind of you to take the time to come and find me," Derry said.

"The number is 555–1066. Can't get any easier to remember than that." He laughed at his own joke. "Are you going to lead me out of this wilderness, Katie, or shall I stumble out on my own?"

"Of course I'll come with you. Sorry to disturb you," she said to Derry.

"You've never disturbed me, Katie Coyle." There was a note of sadness, of tenderness in his voice, which made her pause and meet his gaze once more.

"I'll see you again, Derry." Alistair was already crashing back up the path.

"Count on it." He gave her another wry grin, and turned back to the stones.

"What an unpleasant fellow," said Alistair, as they emerged from beneath the trees. "He's clearly pretending to be something he's not."

"What on earth do you mean?" Katie stared up at him.

"Come now, Katie. I didn't think you'd be the type to be taken in by a pair of blue eyes. That accent is obviously phony. He's no more Irish than I am. And what does he think he's going to accomplish making notes of those markings? The originals have been analyzed again and again."

Katie bit her lip. There was definitely something odd about Derry, there was no doubt about that. For one thing, he'd been dressed in the same pair of shorts and T-shirt as the other night, only this time he'd been wearing a windbreaker that scarcely fit his broad shoulders. At least today he'd been wearing shoes. Shoes which, come to think of it, looked about three sizes too big. "There are lots of amateur historians, Alistair." She glanced at her wristwatch. "Oh, my, look at the time. I'm sorry, but I'm going to be late for an appointment if I don't hurry."

"An appointment? With whom?"

"I've arranged to look at some of the town records with Daphne Hughes. Her last words to me were 'punctuality is the courtesy of kings.' I don't think she likes it when people are late." After her dream last night, Katie was even more determined than ever to try and find out all she could about the history of the property.

"Thanks for the coffee and tour. I'll have to stop by again."

"Oh, please do," said Katie. "Take care, now, Alistair. I'll see you around campus." She felt she should offer to walk him to his car but it really was getting late. "Bye now." With an inward sigh of relief, she watched him saunter across the lawn as if he owned the place.

• • •

Derry watched the two of them disappear through the trees. Even before the man had lied, there'd been something about him that set off every internal alarm Derry had ever had. It was the same as the one that had gone off the day Timothy had introduced him to the man who'd ultimately betrayed them both. He'd ignored it then, to his ultimate peril.

He glanced down at the yellow pad of lined paper and the plastic blue pen Mary had left for him. At least it gave more credence to his ruse. But the only way to tell Katie that Alistair was lying was to tell her the truth. But was it entirely a lie? Perhaps Timothy had been forced to flee to the Continent, but the only price on his head would've been an English price. And he would never have left without Mary and their children—or had he? If that were true, something had gone terribly, terribly wrong. And everything Derry had sacrificed himself for had been for nothing.

The telephone was ringing as Katie entered the house. Inwardly she groaned and checked her watch. So much for being punctual. She picked up the receiver and was surprised to hear her sister's voice. "Meggie! You win the Irish sweepstakes?"

Her sister laughed shortly. "Don't I wish. But I just had to call and tell you what I heard. Remember you were telling me about Alistair Proser? There's a scandal brewing here—Mickey—you know, Tim McKnight—mentioned it to me last night. I couldn't wait to call you."

"What's going on?" Katie sank onto the couch. Daphne Hughes was just going to have to wait.

"Oh, this could be big, Kate. I mean really big."

"Well, are you going to tell me, or are you going to make me guess?"

"He's been accused of fabricating evidence in his last book."

"You've got to be kidding." Katie sat back against the fuzzy afghan.

"Oh, no, I'm not. Mickey didn't know all the details, of course, and I'm not sure that anything is actually going to come of it. It's all supposition at this point, and apparently the person who accused Alistair is a notorious troublemaker. But can you imagine?"

"If it's true? My God." Katie stared out the window. The idea that someone with as many advantages as Alistair Proser would stoop to any kind of subterfuge seemed impossible to believe. "Well, what's happening?"

Meg made a little noise, and Katie knew she'd shrugged and shook her head. "You know how slowly things move. I guess there will be an investigation if this guy Peterson gets his way. But we're talking source documents, Katie. There might be hundreds of them. It might take a couple years just to sift through them all."

"Like looking for a needle in a haystack."

"Exactly."

"Well." Katie checked her watch again. "This is certainly an interesting piece of news."

"I thought you would think so. I didn't think you'd heard about it."

"The thing of it is, though, that anyone who's achieved as much as Alistair has as quickly as he has is bound to have made a few enemies along the way. This could all be a case of academic jealousy."

''Oh, without a doubt. But I'll let you know if there's going to be any formal inquiry. You know, Mickey isn't exactly a fan of his, either.''

''The feeling is mutual.'' Katie rolled her eyes. ''Listen, I hate to brush you off, but I'm late for an appointment. You take care, okay?''

''I will. And you, too. And call me next time, will you?''

Katie replaced the receiver. Despite the time, she sat a few moments, staring out the window. Academic fraud was one of the most serious crimes anyone who even thought of an academic career could commit. It couldn't possibly be true. No one—surely no one as serious as Alistair was about his work—would take the risk. It simply wasn't worth it.

Chapter
Eleven

By the time Katie pulled into the library parking lot, the late-morning sun was high in the sky. She dashed into the library and recognized Daphne Hughes's white head bent over the circulation desk. The woman was stamping books with a loud, satisfying thump. Katie watched as Daphne carefully closed each book and placed it precisely in one of a row of neat piles of books. "Hello, Daphne."

The woman looked up and smiled more broadly than Katie had thought she would have, given the fact that she was almost thirty minutes late. "Well, good morning, Katie! How's your first few days of teaching going?"

"Quite well, thanks. I'm enjoying it a lot. I'm really sorry to be so late. I hope it's still convenient for me to look through those archives."

"Why, certainly." Daphne put down her stamp and closed the inkpad. She beckoned Katie into her office.

"I had you down for eleven. I had John Sneed get those records out for you. Here's the key, and just turn off the light and give me the key when you're finished, all right?"

"No problem." Katie started toward the staircase, but Daphne's voice, continuing the conversation, made her turn back.

"You know, you're the first person since old Ronan to have an interest in those old records. He'd be thrilled to think that someone was living in Pond House who cared about its history."

"I've always been interested in history," said Katie, sidling toward the stairs.

"He'd have been heartbroken when Mrs. Monahan sold it to East Bay. He would never have parted with it—he loved that property too much."

"Well," Katie took a step toward Daphne. "Why didn't she leave it to one of her children?"

"They only had one child—Mary's father. He died in World War Two—never even knew he had a daughter. There wasn't anyone but Mary, and by the time Ronan died, she'd run off to goodness only knows where. And frankly, Mrs. Monahan needed the money. But it was a shame to see the house pass out of the family. Old Ronan sure loved it." Daphne shook her head and would have said more, but a tall, lanky man with white hair dressed in work clothes emerged from a doorway on the other side of the desk and leaned across it.

"I got all the cartons moved, Daphne. Now, what were you saying you wanted done with the flower beds out front?"

"Ah, John. I'll come right out and show you." Daphne gave Katie a bright smile. "Let me know if you need anything, dear. I'll send John right up.''

Katie went up the steps silently, shaking with suppressed laughter. East Bay certainly didn't lack for characters.

She flicked on the lights and settled down in front of the pile of bound leather books. She opened the first. Spidery handwriting, faded with the years, covered the page from top to bottom. It was one of the books that listed the shipwrecks along the coast.

> *August 19, 1886—August Morgan out of London lost at sea. Cargo washed up on Somers Point. No survivors.*
> *August 19, 1886—Arrow out of Boston. Twelve crewmen lost. John McNair, sailor, survivor. George Austin, sailor, survivor.*

Katie shuddered. The details of her dream came back to her in all of their frightening realism: the cold and the water and the crashing timbers as the ship was torn apart. The list went on and on, chronicling disasters at sea. Some lists included the names of the dead as well as the survivors, some only listed the number of those who had died in the waves and those who had managed to live. The recordings were listed chronologically, and she surmised that groups of wrecks meant that there had been a large storm. Or maybe, she thought, it was easier for the chronicler to get the job done all at once.

She skimmed back to the beginning of the book. It began in 1861, far too late to have anything to do with the ghost of Pond House. Carefully, she closed it up and laid it to one side. She reached for what looked like the oldest of the volumes. Its leather cover was cracked with age, and she whipped her head around and sneezed as a cloud of dust rose from the pages when she gently opened it.

Bits of yellow paper flaked away at the edges as she touched it. These records should be better preserved, she thought. Surely there was someone at East Bay skilled in preservation. She would have to inquire at the library. Even if someone had to come from Boston—it would be a shame to have so much authentic history crumble into dust. A wry thought crossed her mind. These were invaluable documents—original source materials that could provide a wealth of information to any number of historians and antiquarians. They deserved to be preserved.

The volume began in 1787, the earliest surviving record of shipwrecks along the shores.

A shiver went down her spine, as it always did when she was confronted with evidence from the past. In all the years she'd studied history, the tangible evidence of lives lived and lost never ceased to fill her with awe. She scanned the list of dates and names.

She paused, reading more carefully. She didn't really have a clue what exactly she was looking for. A notation caught her eye. *Privateer*. Hmm, she thought. That might be as close as she was likely to come to the word "pirate." A map of the coast would help, she realized. She got up with a sigh, ready to ask Daphne for help, and noticed a large map of the town pinned to the wall. Excellent. Just what she needed. She got up, found Pond House, and noted that the beach it overlooked was labeled "Forest Cliff." She returned to the book. There was no annotation where that ship had been wrecked.

She carefully noted the name, *Maggie Moore*, and kept reading.

She'd worked her way through over ten years of disasters when a chill went down her spine. The notation was as bald as any of the others, but there was something about it that made her pause.

October 11, 1799—The Wild Rose of Kerry out of Cork, Ireland. Slaver. All lives lost. Wreckage washed ashore on Forest Cliff Beach.

A slave ship out of Ireland? It was possible, of course, but by 1799 the English slave trade had slowed. What was more likely was that the ship held convicts, bound to Canada as indentured servants.

The memory of the dreams she'd had of the man with Derry's face rose up before her as she stared at the faded black ink. He'd been chained at the wrists. Was it possible, she wondered, that the ghost of Pond House wasn't a pirate captain at all, but the ghost of some poor convict who'd managed to crawl up the beach, calling out for help?

But nothing explained why, in all her dreams, it was Derry who wore manacles on his wrists, his clothes soaking wet. What possible connection could her mind make to him? That was one mystery the old records couldn't possibly help her resolve.

She noted the name, the date, and the originating port, and resolved to call Meg the next morning. Perhaps her sister could access records in Ireland that would tell her what kind of ship the *Wild Rose of Kerry* had really been.

"Katie?"

Katie startled. Daphne Hughes was standing in the doorway, smiling. "I was just checking to see if you were okay. It's after two."

"Oh, my goodness." Katie got to her feet, carefully closing the book. "I'd no idea it was so late."

"No, I figured you'd gotten lost in these old books. Old Ronan was the same way. I could've left him up here for days, I think."

"Thanks. Is there anything I can do—?"

"No, no, John Sneed will take care of everything. Did you find what you were looking for?"

Katie glanced down at the book on the table. "I think I may have. They're very interesting, these old records."

Just as Daphne opened her mouth to reply, a bell rang from somewhere downstairs. "Oh, there's the front desk bell. Just leave everything as you found it, and don't forget the light!"

Daphne was gone before Katie could reply. She straightened the books into precise piles. Although she'd spent more time than she'd expected today, her work had turned up an interesting twist. It might explain the chains on the man in her dreams. But it didn't explain why that man was Derry. Or looked so much like him, she thought as she flicked the light switch and started down the steps.

At the front desk, Daphne Hughes was talking into the telephone while Mary Monahan leaned against the desk. "I'm sorry, could you say that again? Try New York? The public library? Yes, yes, I understand. It is an unusual request. All right. I'll try New York. In the meantime you will keep checking?" She paused long enough to flash Mary a smile. "All right. Thanks again." She replaced the receiver and shrugged. "Mary,

I'm sorry. I think that's the best I'm going to be able to do. Are you sure you need this book?"

"I wouldn't ask you to get it for me, Daphne, if I didn't." Mary glanced in Katie's direction and smiled. "I really appreciate your efforts."

"Hi, Mary." Katie nodded a greeting. "Daphne, I closed the door on my way down."

"Oh, very good." Daphne nodded approvingly and Katie felt inexplicably like a good child. "You turned off the lights?"

"Absolutely. And tell Mr. Sneed I appreciated his help, please."

"Of course. Come back any time. And Mary, I'll let you know about that book as soon as I hear anything. New York, my, my!" Daphne disappeared back up the steps shaking her head.

"Where's she going?" Katie asked as the two women walked out of the library.

"To make sure you turned off the lights," Mary replied with a laugh. "I knew she was going to give me a hard time about that book, but it's out of print and I can't think of any other way to get it."

"What book?"

"It's a book on earth energy. Written in the thirties. I was sure my grandfather had a copy, but I've searched his books high and low and I can't find it. Gram probably got rid of it."

"I can check for it at the university library, if you want."

"Thanks, but Daphne already called over there. Some people call her 'Daffy,' but she's thorough. I know she'll figure out how I can get my hands on a copy somehow. What were you doing?"

"Checking through some of the old town records for more information about Pond House. I found the record of a very interesting wreck. Well, interesting to me, at any rate."

"What was it?"

"A ship called the *Wild Rose of Kerry* went ashore here in 1799. She was listed as a slaver..." Katie paused at the look on Mary's face.

"You found that?" The older woman's jaw had dropped and she was staring at Katie, her surprise plain.

"Well," Katie began, bewildered by Mary's reaction. "Historical research is what I do. Or one of the things, you know. It's such a big part of academics."

"Of course it is," Mary said with a little laugh that sounded nervous. "I'm just so surprised. I had no idea."

Katie stopped next to her car. "I'm going to contact my sister in Ireland. She might be able to discover who was aboard that ship. It seems more likely that the ghost is someone who died in a wreck like that, rather than a pirate guarding his treasure. He is, after all, calling for help."

"Well, that's true." Mary glanced around. "How's teaching going?"

"It's going well. I'm not sure how long I'll be there, but it's going well so far. First-semester freshmen are so eager to please, they're cute." She paused, wondering if she should change the subject. *Oh, why not,* she thought. In for a penny, in for a pound. "I—uh—I was wondering if you and Derry might like to come for dinner some time. I'm not a bad cook, and uh—well, even my twin sister says my food isn't dangerous."

Mary was flushed. "That's so kind of you to think of us," she said slowly. She spoke over Katie's shoulder, refusing to meet her eyes. "I—uh—I would have to check with Derry, though—he's in and out a lot, and I really don't see all that much of him." She glanced at her watch. "Goodness, it's getting late." She backed away from Katie. "I shouldn't be holding you up. Thanks for the invitation."

Katie watched the woman practically run across the parking lot. What on earth could she have said to upset Mary? Was it the dinner invitation? She shook her head and climbed into her car. She'd E-mail Meg tonight. That way, Meg would see it first thing tomorrow, and the time difference wouldn't be a problem. And she had so much reading to do if she was going to stay ahead of her freshmen comp classes. She drove off, still wondering what about an invitation to dinner could have upset Mary so much.

Chapter Twelve

Bay rum filled her nostrils, spicy and sweet and strong, and Katie drew a deep breath. Ordinarily, such a scent would be too strong, but this time it seemed to wrap around her like a caress, wrapping her from head to toe in a secure cocoon.

"Annie."

The voice echoed in her mind, and somehow Derry Riordan was with her, dressed in ragged clothes with chains on his wrists. She stared at him curiously, wondering once again why he was dressed that way, and why he called her Annie. "That's not my name," she said.

"But it was," he replied, and she thought it could be true. "And, oh, how I loved you then."

"Then?"

"A long time ago." In his voice she heard the echo of the years and felt an anguish running through it like *a river, an agony that had gone on for years and years and years.*

"Who are you?" she whispered, holding out her hand.

"I'm Derry," he replied. He took her hand and pressed a kiss into the palm.

Desire sparked through her, sudden and wild and she gasped, even as her fingers tightened involuntarily around his. "But who are you?" she repeated, with greater intensity. "And why are you dressed like that?"

"It's what I wore when you lost me."

"When did I lose you?" she breathed. The scent of his bay rum made her dizzy—or maybe it was the way his body was pressing against hers, lean and hard and insistent.

"A long, long time ago," he said. He released her hand and she sensed that his presence was slipping away, out of her reach.

"Don't go!" she cried.

"You know where to find me," he whispered, and the scent of the bay rum faded, even as he receded into the mists.

Katie opened her eyes. The red numbers on the face of her clock read 4:25. Outside the sky was still dark, and the house was very still. The hum of the refrigerator was the only sound. She turned on her side, drew a deep breath and started. The unmistakable fragrance of bay rum was fading. She bolted upright, her heart beginning to pound. With a trembling hand, she reached over and turned on her bedside light. Shivering, she reached for her bathrobe and pulled it around her shoulders, but she knew the sensation of cold had nothing to do with the temperature. What did the dreams mean?

This wasn't the first time the image of Derry had invaded her dreams. Who was he, and why did he affect her so much? And what on earth did that one mean? Calling her Annie, and telling her he'd known her a long time ago? Why did it seem so real?

She got out of bed, and walked over to the window. She stared into the woods in the direction of the Stones. And why did she think that if she got dressed and went out there right now, he'd be there? Waiting for her?

She shook her head and as she turned away, she caught a glimpse of a flash of white beneath the trees. No, she thought. It couldn't be. No one would be out in the woods at 4:30 in the morning. But even as she told herself it couldn't be possible, some other part of her grew even more certain that Derry did, indeed, await her among the Stones.

She walked into the living room and switched on the light. The floor was cold beneath her bare feet. She sat down at her computer. The keyboard clicked as she typed in the necessary commands. The modem whirred. A white envelope flashed in the bottom right corner of her screen.

Curious, she clicked on it. Although she knew her sister wouldn't have any information for her, at least Meg must've opened her E-mail.

"Hey there," the message read. *"Since when are you so interested in shipwrecks? Is that house you're living in haunted or something?"* Katie smiled. It wasn't the first time that her twin had put her finger uncannily close to the truth. *"I'll do what I can. I'm not sure exactly where to start looking, but a friend of mine is into that*

period. I'm sure he might have a clue where to check.
Heck, if I offer to buy him a pint or two, he might even
do it for me :). I'll let you know as soon as I hear
something. And don't forget, it's your turn to call me
next time!!!! Kisses—Meggie.''

Well, that was that, then. With any luck, Meg might
turn up some information in a week or two. Katie
glanced out the window. Above the brightly colored
trees, the sky was turning a pale gray-blue. A gust of
wind made the branches sway back and forth. Autumn
was definitely in the air. Soon she'd be able to have a
fire. She rose and went to the window. In the early-
morning light, she could see the ripples as the wind blew
across the surface of the ponds. She stared into the trees.
Why was she so certain that if she dressed and went out
into the woods, she'd find Derry already there? What
did her dreams involving him mean? She'd had vivid,
lifelike dreams before, but none quite so . . . quite so . . .
she fumbled for the word. The dreams were real in the
oddest way. Real wasn't how she wanted to describe
them. But ''real'' was definitely the word she kept coming back to. But what were they trying to tell her about
Derry? Or more to the point, what was it that *he* was
trying to tell her? Unlike other dreams, she could remember the details of their conversation with crystal
clarity.

She turned away from the window. Well, she thought,
there was only one way to find out. She'd find Derry
and confront him about it. What was the worst he could
think of her? That she was as crazy as the town thought
Mary to be? Then a thought occurred to her, and she
paused in the act of pouring water into the teakettle.
What if, a little voice whispered from some dark corner

of her mind, what if *he's* not exactly what he appears to be at all?

The noon sun shone through the trees, even though the air that stirred the leaves was chilly. Katie shivered despite her thick wool sweater. If today was any indication, she'd be building a fire by the weekend. She pushed through the trees and emerged into the clearing. She tucked her hands securely into the pockets of her jeans. All around her, the Stones rose like silent sentries. Out of habit, she peered curiously at the writing on the closest one. It meant no more to her today than it had on any of the other occasions she'd examined it. She peered around all the Stones. She was alone.

There was no sign of Derry. She walked around the perimeter, slowly, pacing, pausing now and then to peer at the Stones, gazing from left to right, not certain what she expected to find. A flash of red on the ground by one of the biggest trees surrounding the clearing caught her eye. She hurried over to see what it was.

She reached down and tugged on the fabric, and to her astonishment, a dark-green backpack fell out of a hollow of the tree. She peered inside. The fabric was the sleeve of a navy windbreaker with a red stripe—a windbreaker just like the one Derry had been wearing the other morning. She rummaged through the backpack. Inside, she found the white T-shirt, navy shorts, and faded running shoes he'd been wearing as well. She stared at the clothes. What did this mean? Was he camping here in the woods? She glanced in every direction, but there was no sign of a fire, or anything else that might be a sign of human habitation. She stuffed the clothes back inside the backpack and shoved it into the hollow of the tree. She glanced at her watch. She had about fifteen minutes before she had to leave for the college if she was going to be early for her afternoon class. She really hadn't had the time to come home, but she'd been so eager to find Derry. . . .

She rose to her feet and brushed off her jeans. It didn't matter whether she was few minutes early or not. She was going to call Mary Monahan and try to get to the bottom of this. There was too much about all this that was beginning to seem very strange.

Once inside, she dialed Mary's number on the old-fashioned phone with a trembling finger. She drew a deep breath to steady her nerves, and caught the scent of bay rum. She swirled around, half expecting to see Derry standing beside her, but the room was empty.

Mary answered on the third ring.

"You have to tell me the truth," Katie said, without further greeting.

"The truth?" Mary echoed. "About what?"

"Derry."

There was a silence on the other end of the line.

"I know you told me he was harmless, Mary, and I believe you, but there're too many strange things going on, and since you know him so well, you have to tell me the truth."

"He is harmless," said Mary. "I've never known him to hurt a soul."

"And how long have you known him?" Katie demanded. "I don't mean to sound paranoid, but you've got to understand that I'm out here all by myself. I need to know why you trust him."

"Well, quite a long time, really," Mary said faintly.

"Five years? Ten? Where did you meet him?"

"I—uh—I met him right on the beach. Practically where you and I met."

"That can't be true," said Katie, trying to keep the accusation out of her voice. "He told me himself this was his first visit to the States. How long have you known him?"

"About—well—more than 20 years."

"More than 20 *years*? You've known him since he was a boy?"

"Katie," Mary spoke firmly, calmly. "If there're things you want to know about Derry, I think you should ask him yourself."

"I found his clothes behind a tree out in the woods just now. What are they doing there? Is he camping out or something?"

"Ask him."

"Why won't you tell me?"

"Because he asked me to keep certain things in confidence, and I don't want to violate his trust. But I'm sure if you ask him, he'll tell you anything you want to know."

"Maybe you can tell him I'd like to talk to him." Katie glanced at her watch. It was time to go.

"Sure," said Mary. "I'll be happy to. But don't be surprised if you see him before I do."

Nothing's beginning to surprise me, Katie thought. "I'm sorry to sound as if I doubt you, Mary. I don't mean to."

"I'm not offended. But if there's something you want to know about Derry, you have to ask him yourself. I hope you understand my position."

"Of course," said Katie.

"Why don't you talk to him, and call me back if you want to talk?"

"All right, I will." Katie replaced the receiver slowly. But all afternoon—driving to school, teaching, checking in the office for her mail, and driving home—she wondered again and again what Derry could tell her that she'd need to talk about with Mary.

"You know she's on to you." Mary leaned against the Stones. Derry paced like a caged lion within the perimeter of the Stones. He wore a heavy cable-knit sweater she'd brought him over his ragged clothes. His feet were still bare.

"I never expected she'd go looking for the clothes."

"You didn't put them away very carefully."

"I did! Some animal must have got to them." He stopped the pacing and sighed. "Now what?"

"Tell her the truth."

"How can I do that? She'll think I'm mad."

"She's beginning to think you're a liar. Mad is better than that, at least." Mary cocked her head. He was so damn good-looking. The faintest haze of a beard darkened his chin, and his eyes were bluer than the sky, if such a thing were possible. "And besides, you *are* a ghost. You can prove that."

He groaned. "So she'll think she's crazy."

Mary shrugged. "Maybe initially. But she strikes me as being fairly levelheaded. And she doesn't rush to judgment. I think she'll surprise you."

"I think she's likely to move out of Pond House and never come back again." His lips tightened into a thin line.

"Derry, maybe there's a way."

"A way to what?"

"Release you." Mary rose to her feet. "I've been doing some reading. I think there might be a way to interrupt the field or the energy lines long enough to release your spirit. Why don't you let me look into this? I have some friends who might be able to—"

"Mary, it's not about that." He gave her a look of such raw, savage pain, her heart clenched in her chest. "You know that. I think this woman is Annie come back to me. And I won't be losing her again, do you hear me? I can't. I've spent two hundred years in this . . . this limbo. And now, there's finally a chance of being reunited with her—" He broke off. "I'm sorry. I shouldn't expect you to understand, but I can't bear to think of leaving here and going into some great beyond without her."

"I do understand," Mary said quietly. She pulled her jacket closer, even though the sun was warm across her shoulders. "I think you need to tell Katie the truth, Derry. A lie isn't going to reunite you with her. A lie isn't going to make things easier. The truth might be hard to face for both of you, but in the end it's the only way." She shrugged. "I've given you my best advice."

"And I thank you for it, Mary." A look of regret crossed his face. "I am sorry, you know."

She shook her head. "No more sorries, Derry. And no more lies, okay?" She gave him a crooked smile and escaped into the trees before he could reply.

Chapter
Thirteen

Katie stepped into the clearing, her flashlight clutched in one hand, her heart pounding in her chest. Even though it was nearly six o'clock and the daylight wasn't going to last, she wanted to try and talk to Derry before he invaded her dreams again.

She stood quietly in the center of the Stones, not certain what to do. Finally she lifted her head and spoke aloud. "Derry? Hello? Are you around?"

She waited. Almost immediately, as if in answer, he stepped from behind the Stones. "Hello, Katie Coyle," he said in his wonderfully soft brogue. "I'm very pleased to see you again."

She eyed him up and down. He was wearing black pants that ended at his knees in a ragged hem, and a thick Aran sweater of creamy white wool. His feet were bare. "Hello, Derry."

He didn't reply.

"Aren't your feet cold?" she blurted, finally.

He glanced down, as if surprised to see them. "Perhaps a bit," he said. "But I don't really notice."

There was something double-edged about that remark, something that struck her the same way the things he'd said in the dream did, but he said nothing more and he seemed to be waiting for her to continue. She hesitated for just a moment, drew a deep breath and plunged in. "I found some of your clothes over there," she said. "And I wondered—well, I guess I wondered what they were doing there. Are you camping out here? I asked Mary to tell me what was going on, and she said I should talk to you. She said she wasn't at liberty to violate a trust. And I don't mean to pry, but I do live on this property, and I feel I have a right to know if you've been camping out in these woods."

He waited a few minutes after she finished speaking. He seemed to be considering. "You're right," he said at last. "You do have the right to know what's going on here. I'll try to explain the truth as best I can. Perhaps you'd like to sit down?" With a sweep of his hand, he indicated the mossy ground.

She sank down beside one of the Stones and leaned against it. He began to pace. "What is it?" she asked. "Are you in some sort of trouble? Are there people looking for you?"

"Well, the short answer to that is yes, I'm in trouble, you could say. But no one's going to come looking for me. No one's come looking for me in a very long time."

The phrase reverberated, an echo from the dream. "You said that last night," she said, without thinking. "In the dream, that's almost exactly what you said—" She broke off. Who was crazier here—him or her?

"You aren't crazy, Katie Coyle." He squatted down

beside her and picked up her hand. His touch was smooth and cool. "But what I'm going to tell you will sound bizarre. I only ask you to listen to the whole story before you run away. Is that fair?"

"I—I suppose so." She gently withdrew her hand and sidled a little further away.

He made no attempt to touch her. He rocked back and settled on the ground, his back against a Stone and his feet flat before him. "My real name is Diarmuid O'Riordan. I was born in my father's Dublin town house in the year of grace 1769."

Katie gasped, but he held up his hand. "You promised." She tightened her grip on the flashlight. The shadows were lengthening all around them and the whole atmosphere seemed charge with an incipient kind of energy.

"Go on," she managed.

"My father was also Diarmuid O'Riordan. But he was the ninth Earl of Kilmartin. And I was his firstborn son. When I was eight, my mother gave birth to another son, my brother Timothy. But by that time, I'd been sent to school in England." He took a deep breath and looked away. "Those were troubled times in Ireland." He shook his head. "I don't need to tell you that. My brother fell in with a crowd of rebels who wanted to sever all ties to the English throne, and establish Ireland as a separate, independent nation. They had some support from the French, but—" He broke off once more. "I tried to stay out of it. I didn't really care about their rhetoric. It seemed to me that one government was likely to be as good or as bad as the one before it. I lived mostly in London. We were very wealthy, you see, and my life was . . . easy." He stared into the twilight. "And

then my father died. I came back to Ireland and found
my brother to be heavily embroiled in plots and plans
and revolutions. At first I thought he was a young, head-
strong, heedless boy. And then I came to see that he
believed in everything he spoke of, and that perhaps Ireland and her people would indeed be better off without
the yoke of England.''

Katie leaned forward, listening intently. His face in
the shadows was haunted and drawn, and his voice had
the weight of years.

"Well, things fell apart. Someone—I won't go into it
now—someone betrayed us all. Tim was arrested and
sentenced to hard labor in Australia. But my years in
England stood me in good stead—I had friends, you see,
in very high places. I was given a Crown pardon. But I
couldn't save Tim. He had a wife, and a child. And
another on the way. And he was sickly. There was little
doubt in my mind that if Tim got on that boat to Australia he'd die on the way there, and never come home
again. So I took his place.''

"You did what?" Katie whispered.

Derry laughed without humor. "I thought I'd lost the
woman I loved. Life didn't mean much to me, then. Oh,
I had my life, but it didn't matter. Most of my estates
were forfeit. I felt as though I'd lost everything, and I
couldn't bear to see my brother and his family torn apart.
So I took his place.''

"But you never got to Australia.''

"No. Great storms blew the ship off course, further
and further west, and finally we were wrecked here—
here, on that beach. In that water.'' He raised his hand
and pointed. "I managed to drag myself out of the water
and onto the beach. I was halfway up the path, but it

was cold that night. So cold. And there was no one to hear.''

"And so you're telling me you died?'' Katie leaned forward. "Are you telling me you're the ghost of Pond House? It's you calling in the night?''

He rubbed a hand over his chin. "Indeed, Katie Coyle. That's exactly what I'm telling you. The voice you hear is mine—though it's only an echo from the distant past. There's something about this place that traps energy, all sorts of energy, something about the way the ponds and the water and streams all converge. And here, in the center of the Stones, is the place where it all converges. This is where the power is centered. And this is where I can take on a human shape once more, and be as real as you are.''

Katie leaned back against the Stone, scarcely daring to believe what she heard. "I—uh—I hope you'll forgive me if I say I find all this hard to believe.''

He shrugged. "I've found it hard to believe for the past two hundred years.''

She leaned forward, searching his face in the falling dusk. There was no doubt in her mind he believed that what he was telling her was the truth. "And, um, you can't go beyond the Stones? But I've seen you in the woods, on the beach—''

"There's a circumference of about one hundred yards in all directions where the energy field is sufficient to sustain my form. But once I step beyond it, I just . . . disappear.''

Katie blinked. "So you can move beyond the circle?''

"Yes. But not in my body. Beyond a certain radius, I just disappear.''

"I see.'' She wet her lips. "Can you disappear now?''

"Here?"

"Yes." Their eyes met and held, and a shiver went down Katie's spine. Ghost or no, there was something about this man that touched her in some place no one else had ever reached. He looked so tall and strong, but there was an aching vulnerability about his mouth, and in the twilight his eyes were sad.

For an answer, he whipped off the sweater and handed it to her. "Hold this." She had just enough time to notice the ragged shirt beneath the sweater when, in a twinkling, he was gone.

She gasped. "Derry!" She clutched the sweater, and the odor of bay rum rose from the heavy fabric. "Derry?" She peered around the Stones in all directions.

"I'm here."

She whipped her head back and there he was, in much the same position as when he'd vanished. "My God. It's true."

He gave her a sad smile. "Yes."

"Why—why did you tell me you were staying with Mary? I . . . I . . ." Even as she spoke, she knew the answer.

"What could I tell you? Hello, Miss Coyle. I'm a ghost. Don't worry, I won't harm you. I'm just—how is it said now—hanging out here in the woods. You'll see me from time to time, but think nothing of it."

She giggled in spite of herself. The situation was so absurd. She shivered a little as a cool breeze swept through the clearing. "Oh, here." She handed him back his sweater.

"The clothes disappear when I do, you see."

"Ah." She raised her eyebrows and rocked back, wrapping her arms around her knees. It was getting chilly. And dark. She switched on the flashlight and pointed it to the sky. "You can't come back to the house, can you?"

"Not like this, no. If you're cold, and need to go, I understand."

"No, I'm all right. I'll have to go in a bit, but there's still something I want to ask you. About the dreams."

He looked down. "Forgive me. I . . . I . . ."

"You can do that?"

"Not always. There's only a few times in the night when your mind is open and receptive. But, you see, Katie Coyle, there's something else about you that I haven't told you. You look just like Annie—Annie Malley."

"And she was . . . ?"

A smile swept across his face, a smile of such regret and pure longing that she felt a pang in her chest. "She was the bravest, sweetest, kindest, most loving woman I could ever imagine. I thought they killed her, you see. I thought she was lost. 'Tis another reason I volunteered to switch with Tim. But when I boarded that cursed ship, I saw her on another, and she was swollen with child. And I knew it was mine. We were bound for the same place, you see, and I had such hopes, even in that hellhole they called a ship, that in the end we'd be reunited and we'd make our way back home. But it didn't turn out that way," he finished with a bitter twist to his mouth.

"I'm so sorry," Katie whispered. What else was there to say?

"But you—you have her face. And when I saw you, I thought surely, surely there was a reason for your coming here, of all places. And I saw that you were a scholar of history—Irish history, no less. And I thought perhaps you were Annie, come back to me."

Katie drew a quick breath that caught in her throat. "Oh, Derry." Once more their eyes met, and this time she felt a spark of desire shudder through her. What was it about this man—living or not—that called to her more fervently than any other had ever done before?

He reached out and picked up her hand. Her head jerked up and before she knew it, he had gathered her into his arms. The stark light from the flashlight illuminated the sharp planes of his face, and his eyes glittered. His embrace was strong and demanding, and at the same time somehow comforting. She had just enough time to murmur his name when he bent his head and kissed her.

His mouth was warm and sweet and his lips were firm and insistent. She gasped as passion flooded through her, a hot tide of feeling that engulfed her like a wave. A warning bell tolled in her mind that this wasn't real—couldn't be real—but the feelings were so deep and hot and strong, she raised her arms and twined her fingers in his thick, black hair and opened her mouth to his.

Finally, he drew back. His words surprised her. "Forgive me." He got to his feet and she stared up at him, her heart pounding, her whole body trembling. "Forgive me, Katie Coyle. I wanted to ask for your help."

She stood up a little unsteadily. "There's nothing to forgive. Of course I'll help you, Derry. I'm not sure what I can do, but of course I'll help you. What is it you want?"

His response surprised her. He stared at her a long moment. "I used to think I knew exactly what I wanted," he said at last. "But now I don't really know at all.'' He turned away. ''It's getting late, and it's getting cold. You can't stay out here.''

''We'll talk again tomorrow?'' she asked uncertainly. He nodded, eyes closed. ''Whenever you wish.''

''I'll see you then.'' She picked up the flashlight and turned to go and his voice echoed in her mind. *''And in your dreams, Katie Coyle. In your dreams.''* She turned around, and knew before she did that he was gone.

Chapter
Fourteen

The envelope icon was flashing on her screen when Katie stepped into the house. She sat down at the computer. Her fingers were shaking as she clicked at the keyboard. Get a grip, she told herself. *Get a grip?* the little voice in her mind mocked. *You just spent an hour with one of the best-looking men you've ever met and he just told you he's a ghost. And he made you feel like no one's ever made you feel before. Oh, sure, Katie. Get a grip.*

She silenced the little voice with a will she didn't know she had, and clicked on the envelope.

"Hey, you. My friend came through big time . . . in more ways than one, if you get my drift :). Anyway, here's what he told me. The Wild Rose of Kerry sailed from Cork in September of 1799. She was heading for Van Diemen's Land in Australia with a load of convicts. She never arrived, and she's listed as being lost at sea. If you want more information, let me know. Kisses, Meggie."

Katie stared at the screen. She clicked on the "reply" icon, and typed: *"Thanks very, very much. Is there any chance to obtain a list of the prisoners? I'll call you tomorrow. Kisses, Katie."* She hit the "send" button, leaned back in her chair and folded her arms across her chest. She was going to try and corroborate Derry's story any way she could. He should be able to point her to court documents which, if they existed, might enable her to piece together his fate and that of his family.

She glanced at the clock and sighed. After seven. She should do some reading for tomorrow, but she was too restless. She got to her feet and paced to the window. It was difficult to believe Derry's story, but it certainly explained quite a lot. There was so much she wanted to ask him. It was hard to restrain herself from going back out to the Stones.

The telephone's shrill ring startled her out of her reverie. "Hello?"

"Hello, Kate!" Alistair's voice grated on her nerves, and she closed her eyes. He was the last person she wanted to talk to tonight.

"Hi, Alistair. How are you?"

"Just fine, thanks. Listen, I wanted to know if you were planning on coming to Pater and Mum's shindig this Friday."

"This Friday?" Katie searched her memory, and drew a blank.

"Yes, you must've gotten the invite. It's for the whole department. You wouldn't want to miss it."

"Of course not," Katie said, thinking furiously. There was no question that she had to attend. "Of course I'll be there."

"That's just great, then. We can hang out and have a

drink or two, and then you can make good on your rain check. How's that sound?''

''Oh.'' Katie groaned inwardly. ''Sure, Alistair. That would be fine.'' There was no other way to get him off her back, and this would provide the perfect opportunity to ask him more about his theory on the fate of the Earl of Kilmartin. *After all,* a little voice whispered, *Derry could be lying.*

''The festivities start at five. How's your work coming?''

''Just fine.'' She tiptoed over to the front door, opened it, and pressed the doorbell. ''Oh my, there's my doorbell. I must run. I'll see you Friday, Alistair.''

''Absolutely.''

Katie hung up and sagged. Just what she needed. An evening listening to Alistair Proser expound on his favorite topics wasn't at the top of her most-wanted list.

Idiotic popinjay.

The voice in her mind startled her even more than the telephone had. ''Derry?'' she said aloud. ''Is that you?''

The man's a liar.

''Why do you say that?''

Everything he said the other day was a lie. He doesn't know what happened to me.

''But Derry, perhaps he's found your brother. Isn't it possible he might have assumed your identity, when you didn't return?''

That was impossible. The title was forfeit to the Crown.

''I've started to do some checking on my own. I'll have some answers for you, hopefully soon. And on Friday, when I see that 'idiotic popinjay,' as you so eloquently put it, I'll ask him more about how he reached his conclusions.'' She rubbed her temples.

Thank you.

The air rippled with an invisible energy, and Katie caught a hint of Bay Rum, and felt the slightest pressure on her face. Derry had kissed her cheek.

Within the silent circle, the air was charged with a silent, incipient energy that pulsated to the marrow of Katie's bones. She felt, rather than saw, his hands reach around her and cup her breasts, pressing her back against his chest. He bent his head and nibbled on her ear until Katie sighed with pleasure. She turned in his embrace, and his mouth was warm and welcoming, and somehow, before she knew quite what had happened, they were lying on the forest floor, and the ground beneath her was spongy and soft, and the man above her blotted out the trees and the Stones and the sky. There was nothing in the world but him—his arms and mouth and chest, all pressing her down, and her body felt liquid, as though she melted into him.

And somehow they were one, joined at lips and loins, and they moved together in a timeless, ancient harmony, flowing in and out of each other, as if they had ceased to be flesh at all, and instead were made of something at once far less substantial and far more real.

Her body throbbed with his, and she wrapped her arms around his shoulders, and felt herself dissolve in a burst of heat and light so brilliant, she shut her eyes and knew she cried out his name over and over again.

The red numbers on the clock read 5:16. Katie twined her fingers in the sheets, still breathing hard. Her whole body was quivering, and she pressed her lips together, willing herself to calm down. Her heart pounded audibly in her chest. She sat up. This had to stop. These dreams were too real—too unnerving. She'd dreamed of lovers before, but never had a dream seemed so . . . so genuine. It was as if it were actually happening. She ran her fingers through her thick curls and got out of bed.

The sky was a dark gray. She dressed quickly, pulling on her clothes from the previous day. She made a cup of tea, and carrying the mug and her flashlight, made her way down the path to the Stones.

Inside the circle, she paused. She had to talk this over with him. These dreams couldn't continue. She drew a deep breath. "Derry?"

Immediately he stepped around a Stone into view. He was wearing only the tattered rags of his breeches and shirt. "Good morning, Katie."

"I—I need to talk to you."

"It is a bit early," he said. "Not that it matters to me. But you should be abed, getting your full measure of beauty rest."

"It's a little hard to rest when . . ." To her horror, she felt herself blush.

"When?" He took one single step closer, and she felt her heart leap in response.

She bit her lip. "When you make me dream of you that way. . . ."

"What way?" he asked, his voice not much more than a whisper. In the shadows she could not see his eyes, but his words were as soft as a caress.

"That—that way, when you make me dream of . . . touching . . . and kissing . . . and . . ." She broke off, stumbling over her words, feeling as tongue-tied as a schoolgirl. She took a long drink of her tea and hoped the dim light hid the trembling of her hand.

"I had nothing to do with your dreams last night, Katie." She heard, rather than saw, him take another step toward her. "What exactly did you dream?"

She tightened both hands around her mug. "You didn't?"

"No." He paused. "What was it? Did it frighten you?"

"No—I mean, yes—not really, no, but it was so—so real. So—"

"So?" He was beside her, and he tilted her chin up with the tips of his fingers. "So what?"

She swallowed hard. In the soft gray light of dawn, she could see how blue his eyes were, how chiseled his mouth and cheekbones. The memory of his kiss the day before flashed through her mind and she felt a tingle run down her spine. "So very—"

"Like this?" he murmured, and then he gathered her mouth to his.

She stiffened momentarily, and then relaxed as his arms wrapped around her, drawing her close. Through her thick sweater she could feel his body pressing against hers, and she opened her mouth as he ran his tongue along the edges of her lips.

He reached beneath her sweater and cupped her breast in one smooth hand, rolling the hardened nipple between his thumb and forefinger. She gasped through his kiss, and he raised his head. He only smiled down at her, and bent his head once more.

Somehow the mug was no longer in her hands, and they were lying in the center of the circle, and the mossy earth felt as comfortable as the mattress of her bed. A distinct, damp odor rose from the ground, a green scent that seemed to pulse with that same elusive energy she remembered from her dream.

But she had little time to consider it, for he was above her, and somehow, they were naked, their clothes in scattered heaps, and he was pressing against her, and she was raising her hips to meet him, drawing him deep inside her, until he had buried himself to the hilt in her warm, wet depths.

His face was buried in her hair and one hand stroked her breast while the other caressed her face. She writhed beneath him, her body seeking its own release, and he drew back a little, and laughed softly in her ear, biting the lobe.

She moaned in protest, and he thrust harder. Again and again he drove deep, plunging into the very core of her, and she gripped his shoulders and wrapped both legs around him, her hips undulating against his, until they shuddered together in one last release.

A little while later, he raised his head and moved away from her. He handed her her clothes, and his words startled her. "Forgive me."

"For what?" She pulled her sweater over her head.

"I—I didn't mean it to go so far." He stood up, pulling on his breeches, and she couldn't help but stare at the long lines of his hard-muscled thighs and calves. He turned around to face her, holding the ragged remnants of his shirt.

"I wanted it, too," she said quietly.

"Katie," he sank down beside her, and picked up her hand. "There's nothing I can offer you. I'm as helpless as a newborn baby. I own nothing, I have nothing—I am, quite literally, nothing. I have no right—"

"Derry, I want nothing from you. I'm happy to help

you as best I can, in any way I can. And don't you suppose I wanted this, too?'' She met his eyes and smiled.

He hesitated, then smiled back. ''Ah, Katie. I don't want you to think I took advantage of you in your dreams.''

She laughed softly. ''I think I'm old enough to be responsible for my own dreams.'' She took a deep breath and glanced up. The sky was blue and the light had changed from gray to gold. It filtered through the trees in long shafts. ''It's getting late. I'd better be going.''

''Will you come back?'' There was a plaintive note in his voice that made her long to right whatever wrongs had been done to him.

''Of course I will. Later. After class.'' She picked up her mug and started down the path, and this time when she turned back to wave, he watched her from beneath the trees, all the way back to the house.

When she stepped inside, the clock read 7:10. She put the mug down and splashed cold water from the kitchen sink on her face. She had never experienced anything like that in her life. Just her luck that he happened to be a ghost.

It was after noon in Ireland, she realized. Maybe she could catch her sister. She dialed Meggie's number. On the fourth ring, a deep, masculine voice answered: ''Hello?''

''Hello,'' Katie said. ''Is Meggie Coyle there?''

''Meg's at the library. Is this her sister?''

''How did you know?''

''You sound just like her. I'm Patrick Ryan, a friend of hers. She'll be back by teatime. I'll be sure to tell her you called.''

"Thanks." Katie hesitated. "Are you the friend who has the interest in the late eighteenth century?"

"The one and the same. Did she pass on to you what I was able to find out about that ship?"

"Yes, she did, and I was wondering, if it wouldn't be too much trouble, if you could dig a bit further. I can pay you for your time, if it's a burden."

"No trouble at all, so far. What else can I tell you?"

"Well, you wouldn't know if there was a list of passengers, would you? Some record of who was on the ship?"

"There may be a list," he replied. "But it wasn't a passenger ship. The convicts were considered less than human, you know, and treated accordingly. I doubt there's a list in existence of all the names."

"I was afraid of that."

"Who are you looking for?"

"I'm not sure how the name would be listed. Timothy O'Riordan, or possibly Kilmartin. He was the brother of—"

"The Missing Earl. You think that's the ship he was put on to go to Australia?"

"Yes," said Katie. "I think I found what happened to the ship, though. It's listed in the archives of the town here as a shipwreck. The date of the wreck tallies with the date you gave me for when it sailed from Cork. There were no survivors of the wreck, so I guess it can't be substantiated that the ships are one and the same, but—"

"It's unlikely there were two ships of the same time with the same name out of the same port."

"Yes."

"I'll do some checking. Perhaps in the court records

of the trial there's some mention of the ship.''

"They exist?''

"Oh, yes. They're sketchy, of course. But Timothy O'Riordan was a member of the landed nobility. He was no common rebel. I'll see what I can find for you.''

"Thanks. I really appreciate it. And please, tell Meggie I called.''

"Absolutely.''

Katie replaced the receiver and stood a few moments considering. It would be interesting to hear what Alistair would say. If he would say anything. Somehow, she had the feeling that he was going to be very coy about revealing anything to do with his topic. And she wondered what he'd say if he knew that she was about to begin an informal investigation herself. Somehow, she didn't think he would be very pleased at all.

Suddenly she missed Meg very much. Ever since she'd come to East Bay, the situation had been difficult. First had come Josh breaking up with her, then the obvious hostility from her department chair, and Alistair's unwelcome interest. And now this. She really needed someone to talk to, but who would understand?

She glanced at the telephone. Mary. Of course, Mary Monahan. Hadn't she said she'd be around when Katie needed to talk? That's exactly what I'll do, she decided as she turned on the taps for the shower. I'll call Mary from school today. I could use a sympathetic ear. Not to mention a warm shoulder.

Chapter
Fifteen

"I hope you understand that I felt very bad about deceiving you about Derry," said Mary as she poured milk from a cow-shaped pitcher into her tea. She offered the pitcher to Katie and picked up a teaspoon. "It wasn't my intention to lie to you. But he wanted your help so desperately, and quite honestly, I couldn't think of any way to tell you the truth without you thinking that I was as crazy as everyone wants to believe. So I'm sorry. I hope you can understand."

Katie stirred her tea slowly. She looked around Mary's sunny living room. It was a cozy room, filled with plants and books and candles and dozens of interesting artifacts from what could only be exotic locations. Mary's two shelties lay on the floor at their feet, snoring lazily. "Of course I understand. I can't quite believe it myself. I'm just glad you can reassure me that I'm not crazy. It's just . . ." She shook her head. "I just don't know what to do."

''What do you mean?'' Mary sipped her tea, watching Katie closely.

''I know you aren't going to believe this. But . . . but Derry . . . it's the way I feel—'' She broke off. How could she confide to anyone that she felt herself falling in love with a ghost?

''How does he make you feel, Katie?'' asked Mary softly.

''He makes me feel as though I'm the most special woman in the world.'' She took another sip of tea. ''I can only imagine how crazy that sounds. But there's something about the man—if that's what you can call him. There's something about him that draws me to him—I dream about him, I find myself thinking about him during the day. I know that it's not going to be easy to help him find the information he's looking for, but I don't care. It's like—''

''It's like you're the most important woman in the world. And only you can help him.'' Mary was looking at her with sympathy.

''Yes, that's it exactly.''

Mary sighed. ''Katie, just be careful. I know how attractive he is. And I understand how incredibly vulnerable he can seem. He is vulnerable, after all. Stuck in that place for the last two hundred years—believe me, I can sympathize, too. But the fact of the matter is that he's a ghost. He's not a living, breathing human being. You can't have a future with him—he doesn't have a future. All he's got is this everlasting present. He doesn't change, he doesn't age. He's exactly the way he was when he died two hundred years ago. You've got to keep that in mind.''

''I know.'' Katie plucked listlessly at the embroidery

on the napkin. "And that's the other thing. Right now, if I go ahead and try to help Derry, I'm putting myself in a potentially—well—politically sensitive position at East Bay."

"What do you mean?" Mary frowned.

"Reg Proser's son, Alistair, is applying for a grant— same one I'm applying for, as a matter of fact. Guess what his topic is?"

Mary shook her head.

"The Missing Earl. Diarmuid O'Riordan. Derry."

"Well, wouldn't his research be a help to you? Couldn't you go to him and ask him to tell you what he knows?"

"I introduced him to Derry one day when Alistair happened to drop by unexpectedly. And, well, let's just say it didn't go that well. Obviously he doesn't know what happened, and his theory doesn't exactly paint Derry in a flattering light. Derry called him a liar and an idiotic popinjay."

Mary burst out laughing. "To his face?"

"No, thank goodness. But it wouldn't have taken much, I could see that. The thing of it is, if Alistair happens to catch wind that I'm researching his topic, he's likely to try and make things very nasty with his father for me. He strikes me as the type to play academic hardball."

Mary rolled her eyes. "Well, who says he has to know? Don't tell him. Just try and find out all you can from him, and make sure you get the full story from Derry. Alistair can't have the information too wrong, can he?"

Katie hesitated. "I don't know. I'm not sure what information he has or where he got it, or what his sources are.''

"But you don't trust it?''

Katie raised her head and met Mary's eyes. "No,'' she said finally. "Let's just say that I think a healthy dose of skepticism is good for all avenues of academic inquiry.''

"There's something you aren't telling me, Katie,'' Mary said quietly. She waited a moment, then waved an airy hand. "Don't worry, I won't pry. But if you feel that by helping Derry you are possibly setting up a rivalry with Alistair Proser, my advice is to tread very carefully indeed. Reginald Proser is a very big fish in a very little pond.''

"And I'm a very little fish in that same pond.''

"And the last thing you need to do is get on the wrong side of Reginald Proser. Trust me. I know.'' Mary paused and stared out the window.

"But on the other hand,'' Katie said, "I don't want to let it get in the way of finding out what I can to help Derry.''

Mary pressed a hand over Katie's and when she spoke, her voice was soft. "Just be careful, Katie. Be discreet with the Prosers and don't let Derry steal your heart. Keep it up here''—she pointed to her head—"and not here''—she pointed to her chest. "Know what I mean?''

Silently Katie nodded.

"There's something else I think you should know, though, Katie. There may be a way to release Derry.''

"What do you mean?''

"He's trapped there, you know that? I've been doing some reading. I know you may think this sounds crazy, or unbelievable, but I think there's a possibility that the energy flow could be halted, or at least redirected long enough to allow Derry to move on.''

Katie drew a deep breath. "I suppose that would be the best for him, wouldn't it?" She managed a smile.

"It would be best for all of us, Katie. You, Derry, even me. You understand what I mean?"

Katie nodded and slowly sighed. Of course she knew what Mary meant. The real question was, how would she ever manage to live with it?

"She's falling in love with you." Mary crossed her arms and watched Derry pace the perimeter of the Stones with a scowl on his face.

"And what if she is?" he demanded.

"How you can say that? Have you forgotten your— uh—circumstances, shall we call them? Is it fair to her? She's about to risk her career helping you, did you know that? She could antagonize some very powerful people if she steps on the wrong sets of toes. Or didn't you ever consider that your innocent request just might have ramifications for someone other than yourself?"

Derry paused in his pacing and narrowed his eyes. "What are you talking about?"

"The head of her department—Reginald Proser—do you remember what he did to me? Well, he doesn't like her at all, for some reason, and his son—the one you call the idiotic popinjay, I believe—well, the son is researching your very person for an article or a scholarship or something—the same thing that Katie's going for. And if she steps on either set of toes—the father's or the son's—it isn't going to be very easy for her at East Bay. Do you understand?"

He gave her a stormy look. "No. I don't, really."

Mary shook her head. "It's not your fault. I'm not saying you should know. But now that I'm telling you—" she broke off impatiently. "Derry, don't you see how unfair it is to let Katie fall in love with you? She's only going to get hurt. What can you possibly offer her?"

He raised his face and stared into the trees beyond the Stones. "And how do you think I feel, Mary?"

"Oh, come. Are you telling me you love her?"

"She isn't like anyone I've ever met."

"She isn't your Annie, either."

"She looks so much like her."

"But she isn't. She's not some eighteenth-century rebel; she's a twentieth-century woman—a very well-educated woman who seems to attract the wrong sort of man."

"And what does that mean?" His head reared up and he glared at her with the full intensity of his fury.

"You aren't really a man at all, Derry. You have to accept that. You can't think it's fair that she falls in love with you. You can't let that happen."

"And I ask you again, Mary. What about me? And how I feel?"

"I can't believe you love her. You only think you do. You only love an image—a resemblance. It's not fair to either one of you."

Derry pulled himself up and met her eyes squarely. "I appreciate your concern, Mary. I'll keep what you say in mind. And I'll be careful to caution Katie about undue enthusiasm. But I think it's best left to the two of us to decide what's fair and what's not. At least where it's only the two of us concerned."

"As you wish, Derry." Mary turned to leave, then

hesitated. "I've heard from my friend, Catherine Armstrong. She's the woman I mentioned to you the other day—the one—"

"One of your witch-women friends?" He made a derisive sound then shook his head. "I'm sorry. That was uncalled for."

"It was uncalled for," Mary said. "I'm only trying to help you. Catherine says she thinks she may be able to redirect the energy field long enough to release you. Do you want me to invite her here to perform the ritual?"

"What kind of question is that? Do I want you to invite some stranger here to willingly tear myself from the woman I love?" He raised his hands, then dropped them in frustration. "Surely you see I don't know what to do."

"I see that, Derry. Think about it, why don't you? And let me know what you decide. Just remember, it isn't just you that's affected by all this. Not any more, at least. You have a human being to think about, too." This time she took a few steps down the path, and turned back only when she heard him call after her.

"You think I'm being selfish, don't you?"

She shrugged. "Derry, after all this time, I think you're very confused about what you want. And I think you're very confused about how to get it. That's all." He let her go, then, and she made her way home with a troubled heart.

Katie stared at herself in the bathroom mirror. Her cheeks were flushed and her eyes were bright. *You look like you're in love, Katie Coyle.* What would Meg say? What would her parents say? She shook her head at her reflection. Her family would probably have her committed to a nice quiet institution.

She could feel Derry waiting in the woods. Almost involuntarily, she walked to the wide front window and peered out across the pond. There he was—waiting under the trees, just on the perimeter of the forest. He raised his arm and beckoned.

She pressed her lips together in a little smile. *I'm coming,* she thought. She grabbed a pen and a notebook and with as much decorum as her anticipation would allow, hastened out the door and across the footbridge to where he waited.

"I've missed you," he said, by way of greeting.

She felt the color rise in her cheeks. *Slowly, Katie, slowly,* she cautioned herself. Remember that he's not what he appears to be. "I need to ask you a few things." She held up the notepad. "If I'm going to try to discover what really happened to your brother or his family, I need more details. How much do you think you can remember?"

"I remember everything," he said. He spoke through a tightened jaw, and his eyes were far away.

Katie felt a pang. "I'm sorry to dredge up painful things." Hesitantly she touched his arm and he turned to look down at her, his eyes full of raw pain.

"But it's the only way, isn't it?" He covered her hand with his, and brought it to his mouth. A thrill ran down her spine, and deep inside her, that low feeling of heat he kindled in her flared hotter. He took her face in his hands, and she saw that his eyes blazed with an intensity that took her breath away. "I want you to know, Katie Coyle, that I appreciate everything you do for me. There isn't much I can give you but my gratitude."

"I—I told you before," she said, trying not to gasp. "I don't want anything from you, Derry. Nothing."

"Nothing?" he whispered. Before she could reply, he swept her up in his arms and started off through the forest.

She laid her head against his chest and heard, to her surprise, the beating of his heart. "Where are we going?"

"To a place where time stands still," he answered, smiling down at her. "To the circle of Stones."

She nestled her head against his chest and twined her fingers in the soft cotton of his shirt. A scent rose from him—bay rum and saltwater—and she realized that his clothes smelled of the sea.

Within the shelter of the Stones, he set her gently on her feet and tipped her chin up to his. "Now," he murmured against her ear, his warm breath sending a ripple of delight all the way down to her toes, "tell me—are you sure there's nothing?"

"Nothing but this," she replied, and she wrapped her arms around his neck and eagerly turned her mouth to his.

He crushed her to him, and his lips were hard and hot and demanding. Need coursed through her veins, as urgent as his mouth.

Her knees weakened and his arms tightened around her. Gently he eased her to the ground. He raised his face and traced her features with the tip of one finger. He smiled into her eyes and slid his hand up under her sweater. "You don't wear that—that contraption that binds your breasts?"

"Not—not when I think this might happen," she answered with a grin.

"You're a hussy, Katie Coyle. A shameless hussy, who's no better than she should be, aren't you?"

"That's how you make me feel." She caught his hand in hers and pressed it over her breast. He closed his fingers on the rounded mound, and at his touch, her nipple hardened into a pebbled peak. He pushed the sweater out of his way, and bent his head. He licked the rosy pink tip with a soft, feathery touch, and she groaned and writhed beneath him. He opened his mouth and took the whole nipple in it, drawing it deep, sucking deliciously, until she thought she would go mad with pleasure.

He teased and sucked and stroked both breasts, pausing now and again to shower soft kisses on her lips and throat and face. His hands roamed lower, over her taut belly to the buttons on her jeans. Deftly he opened them, one at a time, and she wriggled her hips as he eased her clothes off.

He drew back long enough to discard his own ragged clothes. She lay on her back, staring at the puffy clouds that floated overhead. A butterfly danced across her field of vision and she raised her arms above her head as a breeze blew softly overhead, raising gooseflesh.

"You're cold," he said as he lowered his body over hers, making her gasp with desire. "Let me show you how I can warm you."

She gasped again as his bare chest settled on hers and spread her legs, inviting him, tantalizing him with the warm, wet flesh between her thighs. "Show me," she demanded. "Show me now."

In answer he plunged into her and she cried out as her body responded with a downpour of fiery sensation. Nothing she'd ever experienced had felt like this. She clutched him close, twining her fingers in his hair, exploring the hollows of his back, as again and again he brought her to the very brink of ecstasy. Her body shuddered of its own accord, and she moaned as wave after wave of pleasure crested through her, flooding her body with delight, melting her bones in a hot tide of passion so complete she sighed in the deepest satisfaction she had ever felt.

A little while later he raised his head and kissed the tip of her nose. "What was it you wanted to ask me about?"

She looked at him, puzzled, and then burst out laughing. "You know very well what it was, Derry. You made me drop my pen and paper, and everything."

"I'm so sorry," he whispered in her ear in mock contrition. "Can you forgive me?"

"If you help me look for my notebook and pen, sure." She took his face in her hands. "I need the information if I'm going to be able to find out anything that might help you."

He turned his head and kissed each hand in turn. "I know you do. Come, we'll get dressed and I'll help you look. And then I'll bare my soul to you, Katie Coyle," he finished lightly.

"It's only fair," she said, reaching for her clothes. "You seem to see right through to mine."

He gave her a long look, and pulled his breeches up. "If only it were so simple, Katie Coyle. If only it could be that easy."

"Catherine says it must be done during the dark of the next moon." Mary trained her flashlight onto Derry's face and shivered as a cold wind blew through the trees.

"What?" Derry stared at Mary as if she'd entirely

taken leave of her senses. "What moon-ridden madness is that?"

Mary wet her lips and mentally counted to ten. He was upset, she could see that, and she wondered at herself for pushing this at him. Was she just the tiniest bit jealous of Katie? she wondered. Brutal honesty forced her to admit that that might be the case. But she remembered how devastated she'd been when the implications of Derry's existence had been made clear to her. What sort of life could Katie have with him? What kind of life did he have with anyone? "Look," she said slowly. "I'm only trying to help you. If you don't want my help, I'm sorry. I won't mention it again." She turned away.

"No, wait, Mary." He sank to the ground, his back against one of the Stones, and shut his eyes. "You just have no idea how difficult this is. Every time I see her, I feel as if I know her—have always known her. She's becoming dearer and dearer to me—surely you can understand that?"

"I do understand that, Derry. Believe me, I do. If you don't want to go through with the ritual, I understand. Only Catherine says it must be done soon."

"Why?"

"Do you want me to explain every detail to you? There's something about this time of year, when the boundaries between the worlds grow thin, and during the dark of the moon, the energies that flow beneath and through the earth aren't as strong as they can be at other times—say, for example, during a full moon. Catherine feels that this would be the most beneficial time to attempt this kind of thing. Or at least the time when it would be most likely to have some chance at success."

"What must she do?"

"We'll call a meeting of our friends—"

"Your witch-women friends?"

"If that's how you choose to characterize us, Derry," Mary sighed, "so be it."

There was a long silence and finally he turned away. "Give me another few days to think about this, all right?"

"All right. But if you wait too long, the opportunity won't present itself for another year."

"I understand." Without another word he vanished from her sight, leaving her alone in the cold, dark night, with only the Stones rising all around her.

Chapter
Sixteen

Katie paused just inside the door. Through the open archway of the Prosers' huge colonial home she could see from the foyer all the way into the living room and beyond to a screened porch. The guests all seemed to be gathered there, and she glimpsed a white-shirted and black–bow-tied bartender. A woman dressed in a black maid's uniform entered the living room carrying a tray and disappeared under another arch, presumably on her way to the kitchen. Reginald Proser and his wife were nowhere to be seen.

Katie squared her shoulders with a sigh and started forward. She'd only taken a few steps when Alistair's voice from above her head stopped her.

"Good evening, Kate."

She looked up. He was bending over the banister, his long, blond hair hanging loose around his face. He appeared to be wearing a loose-fitting silk shirt with huge sleeves. It resembled the ragged remnants of Derry's shirt, and momentarily her heart beat faster as she thought of him. Then the sound of splintering glass and the surprised silence that followed jolted her out of her reverie. "Hi, Alistair."

"Hang on a sec, will you? I'll be right down."

She glanced into the living room. It looked as if everyone from the English department was there. She recognized quite a few graduate students as well. "I should go say hello to your folks, don't you think?"

"If you insist. I'll be right there."

Katie drew another deep breath and continued on her way. The things we do for love, she thought. The babble from the party grew louder as she looked around the Prosers' living room curiously. They certainly did live in elegant splendor. The room looked like something out of *Town and Country* magazine. Threadbare Oriental carpets covered the polished hardwood floors. The ceiling soared at least six feet over her head. The walls were covered with signed prints, and bookshelves dominated one whole wall. Black-and-white photographs in tasteful silver frames smiled back at her. The furniture was over-stuffed and covered with flowered chintz. She felt as though she'd stepped out of Massachusetts and into an English country home. Which, she thought with a wry grin as she stepped past the wide-opened French doors out onto the flagstone floored patio, was almost what she'd done.

"Well, well, Katie Coyle." Terry Callahan's voice boomed just behind her and she turned, startled. "So nice to see you again—I've been meaning to give you a call and ask how things are going."

Katie smiled up at the dean of interdepartmental studies. He was a huge bear of a man, well into his sixties, and his ruddy face was framed by a thick, silver-white mane. "Dr. Callahan. It's very nice to see you again."

"Terry, Terry," he boomed with a wave of his hand. "How are you finding East Bay?"

"I'm really enjoying the students," Katie said with complete honesty. *I wish I could say the same for my colleagues,* she added silently.

"They are a great group, aren't they?" Callahan patted her shoulder. "Every year they amaze me. But I'll tell you what—every year the new faculty amaze me even more. I've heard some very nice things about you, Katie."

"You have?" Katie blinked.

"Absolutely. You're doing just fine, my dear, and don't let anyone"—here he paused and glanced out the French doors to the screened porch—"convince you otherwise. Come, let's go find our hosts, shall we?"

Katie allowed him to lead her out into the crowded patio. A makeshift bar had been set up at one end, and at the other a buffet table held trays of cut-up vegetables and dips and fat wheels of cheese surrounded by crackers. A maid circulated with scallops wrapped in bacon. Katie caught a whiff of the smoky bacon as the tray went by. Her mouth watered unexpectedly.

To one side of the bar, Reginald Proser held court, surrounded by half a dozen graduate students.

"Shall we?" Terry smiled down at her.

The graduate students parted like the Red Sea at their approach. Proser looked up at Katie, and the fleeting expression of annoyance was instantly replaced by a welcoming smile when he saw who stood behind her. "Miss Coyle," he began.

"There you are!" Alistair reached around Callahan to

grab Katie's elbow. "Thought I'd lost you in this mix."

"How are you, Dr. Proser?" Katie managed.

"Listen, Pater," Alistair barged on ahead over her voice, "Kate and I are going out for a bite to eat. She'll have me back before the witching hour, I promise." He tightened his grip on her arm, and before she could protest, practically dragged her away from the group.

Katie barely had time for a weak smile of apology before they were out the door.

"There," he said, shaking out the enormous sleeves of his silk shirt. "Thank God we're out of there."

"Alistair, how could you do that?" Katie said through clenched teeth. "I'd just about said hello to your father, and I hadn't even seen your mother at all. We could've had at least one drink, and circulated a bit. That was rude. I—I—"

"Well, if you wanted to stay, why didn't you say something?"

And cause a scene? Katie retorted silently. She only shook her head and reached inside her purse. "Come on."

"Where are we going?"

"I guess we'll give Chez Yvette another try, all right?"

"Sounds great. Did you make reservations?"

"Uh, no. Do you think we'll need them?"

"It is Friday," he said. "But it's getting to be the off-season. I think we'll be all right," he added magnanimously.

Katie gritted her teeth all the way to the restaurant. When the waitress had set their drinks in front of them, she leaned forward before Alistair could say anything.

"Alistair," she began. "Can I ask you a few questions about your Clancy topic?"

"Oh?" His voice turned cold.

"You know my friend, Derry Riordan? He's very, very interested in your theory. He wanted me to—"

"Funny. I didn't think he seemed all that interested."

Katie shrugged. "Well, trust me, he is. At any rate, there were a few things he wanted me to ask you about—"

"Such as?" He shot her a look filled with such hostility that Katie paused.

"He's not an academic, Alistair. I think it's really fun when someone outside the academy takes an interest in something as obscure and esoteric as the Missing Earl, don't you?"

It was his turn to shrug. "Sure. I guess. What do you want to know?"

"Well, you mentioned that you'd discovered that the Earl had betrayed his brother to the English. Why would he have done that?"

"Kilmartin spent most of his youth in London. He was more English than Irish. His loyalties were clearly on the side of the English. And the brother was a real troublemaker—he was involved with the rebels from the time he was sixteen or so."

"Ah. So this was something personal, between the brothers?"

"Oh, no." Alistair waved a hand dismissively. "Kilmartin was a double agent for a time. In the end, it's what saved his brother's neck, you know."

"But I thought you said that the estates were forfeit— that the Kilmartin estate was sold to the Church and remains Church property to this day? Why did that happen if Kilmartin was a loyal subject?''

"For show, of course. The Irish would've killed him.''

"And what about his title?''

"It was stripped—again for show.''

"You found court records of all this?''

"I didn't say that.'' He was looking at her with outright suspicion. "I pieced this all together over a very long period of time.''

"I see.'' Katie sipped her drink. "But why do you suppose he didn't go back to England? If he'd acted in the best interests of the English—''

"The Irish had a price on his head. Where do you suppose he'd have been safe? He had to disappear.''

"And where do you think he ended up?''

"Germany. As a minor attaché of the British ambassador. He was very popular with the ladies.''

"And there are records of him there?''

"Well, not specifically, no. His Kilmartin identity was obliterated. It took quite a bit of sleuthing to connect the two together, actually. But it's quite clear once you've done the work.''

"So, if you don't mind my asking—''

"Actually, I do mind your asking,'' he interrupted. "If this friend of yours is so interested, he's just going to have to wait until my article is published. I don't see us talking about your topic.''

Katie sat back. *That's because you've never asked about my topic,* she wanted to scream. But there was no point antagonizing him. "It's just that I find this remarkable, Alistair. It's like the Princes in the Tower, or what really happened to Anastasia. These historical mysteries aren't just popular within the academy. The general public is interested in them as well.''

"I know." He preened. "I'm expecting a book contract out of this, actually. Historical nonfiction, of course, but with a popular slant. Something the general reader will be able to appreciate without having to think too hard." He laughed, a short, nasty sound that made Katie fight to keep her expression neutral. "Can't have that, you know.''

"Can't have what?"

"The general reader thinking. Too much work!"

"I don't know about that," Katie murmured, more to herself than to him.

Predictably, he ignored her comment. "I'm anticipating some controversy, too, of course. The trouble with so many in the academy is that they insist on thinking in the same box."

"I'm not sure it's just that," said Katie slowly. "New theories need to be tested."

He shrugged. Mercifully, just as he had opened his mouth, the waitress set their plates in front of them.

"Oh," said Katie. "This looks great. I'm so hungry I could eat a horse!" She dug into her food with feverish abandon, hoping to forestall the conversation for a short time, at least. She was gratified to see Alistair give her a weak smile and pick up his fork. Maybe she could convince him to make it an early night.

It was later than she'd hoped it would be when Katie finally turned her key in the lock and stepped into the living room. Instantly the scent of bay rum surrounded her, and she felt an overwhelming rush of warmth and welcoming and love. "Derry," she said aloud, smiling. "I'm glad to be back, too."

Come to the woods.

"Now?" Automatically she glanced outside. The night was cool, and very dark.

I have a surprise.

"All right." She dropped her keys on the table and left her purse on the couch. She picked up her flashlight from the coffee table. She'd have to remember to stock up on batteries.

She followed the heavy fragrance out the door and across the bridge, the beam of light bobbing ahead. At the very perimeter of the forest he coalesced into sight and caught her in his arms. "I missed you," he murmured, as his mouth came down on hers.

She barely had time to smile in response. She wrapped her arms around his neck, and gave herself up to the pleasure of his kiss.

He broke away just as her knees were beginning to weaken. "Not yet." He grinned down at her, his teeth even and white in the dark. "Come."

He led her through the woods. Up ahead, she saw an orange glow among the trees. "What's that?"

"You'll see."

They stepped into the clearing of the Stones, and in between the dark shapes, she could see a bonfire dancing and crackling. Smoke rose in a lazy spiral to the sky, and a log split with a hiss and a crack and a shower of sparks. The scent of the fragrant wood mingled with the odors of the sea and the damp leaves. She breathed deeply as he led her into the circle. "Oh, Derry, it's quite beautiful."

"And warm, you see." He slipped his hands beneath her jacket.

She turned, allowing him to undress her. The fire gave off an uneven heat that swept across her in waves. His fingers on her bare flesh burned, and the cool night air made her nipples stand erect and raised gooseflesh on her arms and shoulders.

"You're cold," he whispered. "Come here." He led her to a blanket spread out on the ground. It was soft and smelled of lavender. She looked at him, puzzled. "I borrowed them from Mary." He shed his clothes in a few quick motions and stretched out beside her, pulling the second blanket over them both. In the firelight, his skin was luminous and his eyes were so deep a blue that they almost seemed black. He wrapped his arms around her and pulled her close.

She gave a long sigh and surrendered to his embrace, her body aching with a sudden fierce need. Later, as they curled up together, lying on their sides, watching the fire, she gave another sigh, this one of satisfaction. "This is very nice."

"Yes," he said. "Very nice indeed."

She turned on her back and smiled. "It's like a dream, all of this. You being here—the way you make me feel—I can't quite believe it's all really happening."

"And how do I make you feel?" He wrapped one curl around his forefinger and allowed it to spring back.

"As if I'm the only woman in the world," she said. "You listen to me, you talk to me as if you care about what I say. You make me feel safe and loved—" She broke off.

"I do love you," he whispered.

She rolled to face him. "You mean that?"

"Of course I mean it." He raised her chin and gently met her lips.

"I nearly forgot to tell you," she said. "I had dinner with Alistair tonight. His story is certainly different from yours."

"He's lying," Derry said fiercely.

"He gave me a couple of clues, though. Not a whole lot, but enough to check a few things out. I think it's likely he's found your brother—"

"My brother was no traitor."

"Well, perhaps not, but he could have gone to the Continent. Maybe he did end up in Germany."

Derry made a little noise of disgust, picked up a twig and threw it into the fire.

"I'll start looking into it tomorrow." She yawned. "Oh, I'm tired. I should go."

He gathered her into his arms, cradling her head on his chest. "Not yet, careen. Not yet."

With a little sigh, she relaxed. Her head drooped and her breathing deepened. In a few minutes, she was fast asleep.

Derry lay holding her close, listening to her breathe. Her body was warm and round and firm, and her heart beat in slow, steady beats. Her breast fit snugly in the palm of his hand. He looked down at her face, so vulnerable in sleep.

What was he doing, the voice of his conscience whispered. How was it fair to her, to fall in love. He could offer her nothing—not even a roof to shelter her or a bed to lie on. He had nothing but a borrowed blanket and a fire in the woods.

He buried his face in her curls and the fragrance of

lilies and lavender and roses filled his nostrils. He breathed deeply, relishing the scent.

Maybe Mary was right, he thought with a pang of regret. He had nothing to offer this woman but love. *But I cannot lose her again,* his mind screamed. *She is dearer than life to me.*

You don't have a life, the voice of his conscience retorted. But she does, and she's in danger of wasting it on you. Let her go.

He tightened his arms around her. Let her go. The very thought made him ache. Once again fate had done nothing but play a cruel trick on him. What kind of God had condemned him to this half-life, half-death existence? And what had he done to merit such a punishment? He lay for a long time, watching as the flames slowly faded, and felt as though every chance he'd ever imagined for happiness was dying away with them.

The morning sun glittered on Mary's bracelets as she bent to pick up the folded blankets. Bits of leaves and tiny twigs clung to them, and she shook them out, brushing away as much debris as she could.

"I'll do it."

Derry's voice behind her made her jump. "Damn it, Derry, how many times must I tell you not to do that?" She turned to face him, her heart pounding. The early-morning air was crisp, and he was wearing the old windbreaker that had belonged to her father.

"I'll do it."

She saw at once that he was upset. "Are you sure?"

"Summon your witch women."

"Are you sure this is what you want?"

"Of course it isn't what I want, Mary. But what I

want hasn't seemed to enter into anything for the last two hundred years. I've learned to expect nothing. And nothing—maybe at last—is what I'll get.''

''Oh, come, you don't believe that. . . .''

''What do you expect me to believe, Mary? In heaven or in hell? This everlasting nothingness has been more hellish than anything I ever imagined. And then, at last, *she* comes back to me, and it's becoming so painfully, terribly clear to me that there is nothing I can give her but grief and heartache and emptiness. You think I can believe in a God who would ordain such a thing?''

Mary made a little gesture. ''Maybe not in the Christian God, Derry, but perhaps—''

''In your higher power?'' He turned away with a muttered curse. ''Summon your friends, Mary. We'll have this done. And the sooner the better. My existence here is nothing but pain—for me and anyone who would know me.''

Chapter Seventeen

The telephone began to ring just as Katie turned the lock in her office door. The key stuck in the old lock, and she fiddled with it. Though what was the rush? she wondered, as she reached for the receiver. It was probably Alistair calling for another date. Today was Wednesday, and she hadn't heard from him since she'd dropped him off on Friday night. "Dr. Coyle."

"There's no need to rub it in that you finished first."

"Maggie?" Katie grinned. "What are you doing calling me here? How did you get this number?"

"I called the university switchboard and asked for it, of course. How're things going?"

"Oh," Katie said with a sigh. She shoved the door closed and sank down in the battered chair behind the scarred metal desk. "I seem to be scoring points at every turn."

"Why? What's going on?"

Briefly, Katie outlined what had happened at the Prosers' party on Friday. "And that's not the worst of it. I managed to make Alistair annoyed as well."

"What do you care about that? I thought you couldn't stand the guy?"

"I can't. But his father's my boss. I didn't think it was good politics to annoy both of them."

"Oh. Well, I guess you're right about that. But what did you do to annoy Alistair?"

"I asked him too many questions about his Clancy topic, I think. For someone whose favorite topic is himself, he's pretty closemouthed about it. Tell me, have you ever heard more about those accusations?"

"No, not a word. What's the topic?"

"The Missing Earl. If I didn't already have a topic of my own picked out, I'd write a rival paper."

"You would?"

"Well, sure. In for a penny, in for a pound. But at this point, it wouldn't make sense. I can't afford to come to Ireland to do the research. I just don't have the time, and I sure don't have the money."

"Hmm. That's all that's stopping you?"

"Well, that and the fact that when it came out it would antagonize my department chairman's son. And possibly old Reg, too. You wouldn't believe how much he dislikes me."

"Oh, sure I would," Meg said breezily. "I had to share a room with you, remember?"

"Gee, thanks."

"Hey, what are sisters for? But I have an idea."

"You do? About time."

"Ha ha."

Katie grinned. She'd forgotten how much she missed Meg's banter.

"But, listen," her sister continued. "Patrick was saying how much he'd like to apply for the Clancy, but he couldn't think of anything worth doing. If you collaborated with him—"

"He'd be interested?"

"Well, I can ask him. And have him call you if he thinks he'd be interested. He's here. He can do the research. You'd have to do the bulk of the writing of course, and let him edit it. That would only be fair."

"Oh, I agree," said Katie. "When can you ask him?"

"Tonight?"

"Sounds great to me. Are you sure he'd be interested?"

"Of course he would be. This sort of thing is right up his alley. I guess my only question to you is, why are you?"

"Why am I what?" Katie hedged.

"So interested. You always said the world after 1700 was a black hole as far as you were concerned. I guess I don't understand why you'd want to put all this time into something that really isn't your area."

"Well," Katie said, thinking furiously. What was she going to tell Meg? *It's like this, sis,* she could imagine herself saying. *I met this guy and he's an absolute dream. Only problem is, he's a ghost. And he wants my help to try and get out of the influence of a bunch of Standing Stones that some crazy old coot erected on a site on the property where I'm living.*

"You know," Meg was saying, without waiting for a reply, "I've had this feeling all along that there's something you aren't telling me. Are you holding out on me?"

"No, of course not." Even as she said the words,

Katie could feel herself cringe. She'd always been a lousy liar, especially where Meg was concerned. Her sister could tell by one look whether she was telling the truth.

Fortunately, Meg's radar didn't seem so effective long distance. "Hmm," was all her twin said. "I'd hate to think that there could be anything you wouldn't tell me. But I guess I'll just have to believe you. For now."

"Will you talk to Patrick?"

"As soon as he gets home."

"Home?" Katie raised her eyebrows and let her voice rise in an imitation of their mother. "Who's holding out on whom here?"

"Oh, didn't I tell you we decided to live together?" Meg asked innocently.

"No, you did not. Do Mom and Dad know?"

"Well . . ." This time it sounded as though her sister was doing some mental somersaults. "Not yet."

"And when do you plan to tell them?"

"Well . . ." There was another pause. "Not just yet."

"Hmm." Katie let her sister squirm for a second longer, and then she laughed. "Your secret is safe with me. But you will let me know what he thinks, one way or the other?"

"Of course."

After a few more exchanges, the sisters said good-bye. Katie grinned as she replaced the receiver. It was amusing to think that Meg, who'd always been the good one, had something she'd rather not let their parents know. Not yet, of course. Katie was still chuckling to herself all the way to her car.

As she reached the faculty parking lot, she saw Alistair striding along the street, holding a manila envelope. He didn't look very happy. And he didn't appear to notice her, either, because he didn't acknowledge her with so much as a glance in her direction. If he was still annoyed with her about Friday night, it wasn't going to compare with how angry he'd be if he got wind that she'd decided to write a paper on the same topic. She turned the key in the ignition. It might be the kiss of death to her career at East Bay, she thought. Better that Alistair not know. And if it happened that she won, what could he do about it then? Somehow she thought that the prestige of the award would outweigh his father's disapproval. The worst Alistair could do was challenge her conclusions. And that sort of challenge was expected, and even welcomed. She was confident that with Derry's help, she'd be able to prove her points.

But in the interim—she drove away, frowning, considering. In the interim, it wouldn't be a good idea to alert Alistair. And there were sure to be materials she'd need, books and so on she'd have to check, just to be thorough. How could she get what she needed without him knowing? She drove slowly down the street, turning the idea over and over in her mind.

A blue library sign caught her eye. She was nearly at the intersection that would take her into town if she turned right. Katie slowed to a stop at the red light. She put her right-turn blinker on. Daffy Daphne Hughes might be just the person she needed to talk to.

"I'm glad you've finally come to your senses." Mary watched Derry pace around the perimeter of Stones like a caged beast. Although his words were those of resignation, he appeared to be anything but resigned.

"It isn't a question of understanding." He paused,

facing away from her, and spoke over his shoulder. His face was shadowed, his eyes dark pools of pain. "I know what I am. I know what I can and cannot do or be. But the thought of giving her up . . ."

"Derry, it's the only way. How can she ever be happy with you? Do you want things to come to the same end they did with us? Eventually she'll figure out that there's nothing here—"

He swung around with a ferocity that made her jump. "I want you to try and do whatever you think you can. I want to leave this cursed place."

Mary gave him a long look. "If you're sure that's what you want. I want you to be sure. I've talked to my friend, Catherine. She's fairly certain it can work. The time has to be right for it. She's doing some research now, but I think, just from what I know, that it will have to be soon."

"She'll do it here?"

"Not within these Stones, perhaps. The energy may be too strong here. But perhaps on the periphery, down by the beach—maybe where you died originally—we can hold the earth energy back long enough—"

"Long enough to release me?"

"Yes." He was silent for a long time, and finally she said: "Is that what you want, Derry?"

"I don't know what I want." There was a bitter twist to his mouth as he spoke. "It would be easier for Katie if I moved on."

"It would be better for the two of you if you moved on. You aren't really a part of things here, Derry. You need to go on, to move on to the next level of existence. It's only an odd series of circumstances that's kept you here all these years. Don't you think Katie wants the same? Isn't that what you asked her to help you do?"

He drew a deep breath and spread his hands wide. "I don't think I remember what I asked her."

"What will you tell her?"

He resumed pacing, and she was reminded of a caged tiger. "I don't know. I'll think of something. It will have to be soon, though. Each day that passes it grows more and more difficult to think of giving her up." He ran a hand across his chin. "It would be better if I could convince her to give me up herself."

"And if you can't?"

"I'll think of something." He raised his head and stared into the trees, in the direction of the beach.

Mary straightened. "I got a couple books from England yesterday. I'll call Catherine and talk to her some more. We may have to call in a few of our other friends to help us, you understand?"

"Do whatever you feel you must, Mary." He didn't turn around or look at her, merely walked away into the forest, his shoulders rigid with despair.

She checked the impulse to call after him, to offer a word of sympathy and support, and only slipped away beneath the trees as silently as he.

"I need your help, Daphne." Katie paused and met the older woman's keen gaze with an even stare of her own.

Daphne pursed her lips as if considering. She gave a short nod, reached under the circulation desk and set her bell on the counter. "Come into my office, my dear." She indicated a ladder-back chair that was set at a precise right angle to her own immaculate desk. "Sit down and tell me."

Katie folded her hands in her lap, feeling more and

more like a child approaching the school principal. "I'm working on a project, and I need to do some research, but . . ." She hesitated and Daphne looked puzzled. "I need your help."

"What can I do?"

Katie took a deep breath. "The thing of it is this— the article I'm working on may potentially step on a few toes at East Bay. It's nothing illegal, or immoral or anything like that—"

"It's just that you don't want to risk offending someone over there before you're ready to publish your results?"

"Exactly." Katie gave the older woman a grateful smile. "In order to get the information I need, I was wondering if you could run interference for me, so to speak. If you would contact the library, for example, and request the information, I could retain my anonymity a bit longer than I would be able to otherwise."

Daphne steepled her fingers and frowned, considering. "I can try that. You know, though, that as a professor, you have much more clout over there than I do."

"I'm not a professor yet. Really, I'm not much more than an instructor. And it's more important to me that I have access to the materials I'm going to need without anyone knowing that I want them, than the convenience." Although time was running out, thought Katie.

"I suppose we can go to another library if East Bay won't cooperate," said Daphne. "I'll see what I can do. Is there a list you'd like me to request?"

"Not yet," said Katie. "I'm still working on it. But I'll bring it by tomorrow or the day after at the latest. I need to get working on this."

"Yes, you do that." Daphne paused. "Can I ask what the topic is?"

"Sure," said Katie. "Have you ever heard of the Missing Earl?"

Daphne frowned and shook her head. "No, I can't say I have."

"He was an Irish lord at the end of the eighteenth century who got involved in the Rebellion of 1798 and disappeared—literally just vanished from the pages of history. No one knows what happened to him."

"And you think you might?"

I know I do, thought Katie. But all she said was, "I have a theory. If I can make a strong enough case—"

"It will go a long way toward helping your career?"

"Yes," Katie nodded.

"Well, Katie Coyle, you can count on me to help. As I said, I may not be very effective. But we can sure try." She raised her head and beckoned to someone outside the office. "John Sneed! John! Don't move anything until I get there." She rose, and Katie got to her feet as well. "You'll have to excuse me, my dear, but I really must tell John where I want the chairs in the meeting room arranged. He has his own ideas about things sometimes." With a smile and a wave, Daphne was out the door, shouting, "John Sneed!"

Katie grinned. Somehow she had the feeling that Daphne Hughes was going to be a very effective ally. She was certainly a woman who knew what she wanted. And God help anyone who got in her way.

Derry braced himself. He could feel Katie moving closer, her heart pounding in eager anticipation. She was going to be very angry with him and very hurt. But there was simply no other way around it. If he was going to extricate her from the morass of their involvement, he was going to have to find a way to make it possible for her to accept what he knew was only inevitable.

She burst into the clearing with a smile on her face. "Derry!"

Immediately he stepped into view from behind one of the Stones. "Yes?" He kept his voice neutral, but he could see the flicker of hurt in her eyes, as she registered the change.

"Are you all right?" She stopped short about six feet away.

"I'm fine. What is it?"

Katie glanced from left to right, as though not quite sure she was hearing correctly. "Are you sure you're all right?"

"Of course I'm all right. I never change. What do you want?" He tried to soften the tone in his voice, but he could see the growing hurt and confusion spread across her face.

"I—I came to tell you that I'm going to work on your—your history for my paper. My sister has a friend in Ireland who she's pretty sure will collaborate with me, and I've worked it out with the town librarian that I can use the library as a cover, so it won't cause any conflicts with Alistair or his father. I'll probably be able to tell you something definite by Christmas."

Derry shook his head and backed away. "Christmas?"

"These things take time, Derry. I can work as fast as I can, but there're no guarantees. But the deadline for the Clancy is January, so—"

"That's what I've become to you? A paper?" He

hardened his expression and forced himself to look beyond the now obvious hurt look she wore.

"No! Not at all. How can you say that?"

"It sounds as if that's what you have in mind."

"Well, it is, but how else can I help you? What more do you expect me to do? At least initially?"

"I didn't expect that you'd try and use my predicament as a way to make a name for yourself."

"Make a name for myself?" She was rigid with shock. "Do you have any idea how much time and effort this is going to take? I have two people already who are going to have to put their time and energy into it, as well as—"

"Then I'm sure your project will be a great success." He turned around.

She ran across the space between them, and grabbed his arm. "Why are you angry, Derry? I thought you'd be thrilled. I thought you'd welcome—"

"Welcome my life and my misfortune revealed to all the world? Yes, I'd like to know what happened to my brother and his family. And to my Annie. But I never thought you'd use it as a way to further your own career."

"I—I can't quite believe you're saying this."

"Believe it." Without another word, he stepped behind the Stones and forced himself to disappear. He fled to the beach before he could hear her soft, stifled cries.

Chapter Eighteen

Katie stumbled back through the woods. She felt as though he'd slapped her, or poured a bucket of freezing water over her. What in the name of God had precipitated that? He was nothing like the man she'd thought she'd known.

But that's the point, that same little voice whispered. *He's not really a man at all. And how long have you known him? A month? Six weeks?*

The flashing light on her answering machine caught her eye, and she was tempted to ignore it. But force of long habit made her press the button. A masculine voice spoke, a voice that sounded so much like Derry's with its soft brogue that her heart clenched painfully in her chest. "Good afternoon, Katie Coyle. Patrick Ryan here. I wanted to let you know I'd be happy to collaborate with you on the project. I'm sending you an E-mail with a few ideas I've had. If you have anything you'd like to send me, please do. Otherwise, why don't you call me tonight before midnight? I believe that would be about six o'clock your time. Speak to you soon.''

The machine whirred and clicked as the tape rewound. Katie glanced at the clock. It was just four. She had plenty of time. Was it even worth it, becoming embroiled in such a project, if Derry didn't care? Or if Derry believed she was only using him to further her career? How could he think so?

Tears filled her eyes and she blinked them away. What could have happened to make him so angry? She racked her mind, thinking furiously. She'd done nothing—of that she was quite sure.

With a shaking hand, she dialed Mary's number. When the woman answered, she spoke as calmly as she could. ''Mary, I—I need to talk to you.''

There was a soft sigh at the end of the line. ''Of course. Is anything wrong?''

''It's Derry. He's—uh—he—'' She broke off as a lump in her throat made speech impossible.

''I'll come right over.''

Katie went to the window and stared out over the ponds. The late-afternoon breeze rippled across the water, and the waterfall bubbled beneath the footbridge. Outside, nothing had changed, but it seemed as if a cloud had covered the sun, diminishing the quality and the intensity of the light.

In a few minutes, she saw Mary emerge from the path beneath the trees, cross the footbridge and walk up the graveled path to the front door. Katie opened the door and forced a smile.

''Katie?'' The older woman's voice was soft with sympathy. ''What's wrong?''

Katie forced herself to take a deep breath. "Would you like a cup of tea?"

"Sure. But can't you tell me what's wrong first?"

"It's Derry. He's furious with me. And I don't understand why. I almost get the impression he doesn't want to see me again."

The older woman enfolded her in a warm hug. "I'm so sorry. Come, let's have some tea and talk."

Katie walked into the kitchen, filled the kettle and set it on the stove. "I went out to see him this afternoon as soon as I got home. I wanted to tell him that I've decided to switch my topic for the Clancy grant. I'm going to write about him—to reveal the truth, somehow. So whatever Alistair Proser is going to write won't be the end of it—Derry won't be branded as a traitor or a double agent or worse. And when I got out to the Stones, he was so completely different—"

"Wait," Mary held up her hand. "What are you talking about? Who's branding Derry a traitor?"

"Alistair Proser. He's the son of my department chair, and already has an international reputation as a top scholar. He's got some idea that Derry was a double agent for the British during the Rebellion of 1798 and betrayed his own brother. And that's why he disappeared from history—he had to go into hiding because the Irish had a price on his head—"

"That can't be true."

"Of course it isn't true," Katie said. "Only goodness knows how Alistair has put this all together. And I wanted to set the record straight, before it could even be established as the record—do you understand what I mean?"

Mary nodded soberly. "I think I do."

"But in order to do this—to publish a rival paper at the very same time as someone like Alistair—well, it isn't going to be easy, you understand? I have to be careful—I can't let Alistair or his father know, because you've seen how Reg Proser feels about me. So I wanted to tell Derry what I decided, and I went out there, and it's like he's a stranger. He accused me of using him as a means of furthering my career—and that's not my intention at all. If anything, if I go ahead with this, I'm potentially jeopardizing my career. Reginald Proser is watching me like a hawk. He doesn't like me and he'd leap on any excuse to get rid of me—"

"Katie, I'm sure it's not that bad, is it?"

Katie shrugged. "I've seen what academic enemies can do, Mary. It's not pretty." She busied herself getting out mugs and plates and spoons. "But that's not what's upset me. It's Derry. He's acting like a stranger. Worse than a stranger. He's angry at me. For no reason." Tears filled her eyes again and her voice shook.

"Ah, Katie." Mary patted her back. "Can't you see? He's not really angry with you. He's just trying not to let you get attached to him. Can't you see that?"

"What do you mean?"

"Katie, why do you think I left East Bay? Oh, there was that trouble with Reg Proser, that's true. That was part of it. But that wasn't all of it. Mostly it was Derry."

"Derry?" Katie paused in pouring milk into a little pitcher.

Mary nodded and there was a deep sadness in her eyes. "Come on. Let's have our tea."

Katie placed the mugs and saucers and sugar on the tray and carried it out to the living room. She placed it on the coffee table. When they were settled with steaming mugs in their hands, she turned to Mary. "Can you tell me what happened?"

"Of course," said Mary. "It was so long ago, now. But it always seems like yesterday whenever I see him. He hasn't changed at all, of course. He's exactly the same as the day I met him on the beach when I was sixteen."

"Sixteen?"

"I grew up in Pond House, you know. My father had died in World War Two—didn't even know he'd had a daughter. My grandparents took me in after my mother died. And I guess I always knew as a child that there was something different about this house. My grandfather knew all about Derry, you see. Every once in a while, I'd nearly catch them together. Made me extremely curious, I can tell you. And then one fine September day, much like this one, right after I turned sixteen, I was sitting on the beach, and my grandfather and Derry walked out of the woods. I'm not sure who was more startled—me or my grandfather. But he introduced us, and said Derry was just a friend from Ireland, and ordered me back to the house. Well, after that, I haunted the woods—if you'll pardon my expression. And inevitably, I suppose, Derry came and talked to me. He was lonely, and so was I. I was always a little bit different from the other kids, you see. And my grandfather's reputation didn't help.

"So anyway, we got to be friends. And then, less than a year later, we got to be more than that." Mary looked down at her lap. "I'm not sure how he felt about me. But I loved him with every ounce of passion in my schoolgirl soul. I even went to East Bay because I couldn't stand the thought of leaving him. And then there was the trouble with Proser, and it was becoming painfully obvious, even to me, that there really wasn't much point in the relationship. It couldn't even be called a relationship. What could we do together? There wasn't a shred of normalcy to it. And so even though it tore me apart to do it, I left East Bay. And I didn't come back even when my grandfather died. That infuriated my grandmother, who promptly wrote me out of her will. But my grandfather had left me some money, and so when I decided I could finally risk coming back, I had enough to do what I pleased.

"But I don't think I could've come back to Pond House. I wouldn't have come back here at all."

Katie took a sip of tea. Mary's face was soft and far away. Clearly, she had loved Derry very much. "Do you still love him?"

Mary shrugged and faced her with a sad little smile. "Once you love someone, can you ever really stop completely? Don't you think there's a part of you that just keeps loving that person, despite what grief they cause? Derry was my first love. I don't think I'll ever be able to get over him, really. But I can tell you this. He does love you, Katie. He's spoken of you in a way I've never heard him talk of anyone. And when he's thinking of you, it's as though no one else exists. If he's told you he's angry with you, trust me, he's only trying to protect you. He's only trying to make things easier for you."

"Protect me? From what?"

"From being hurt. From coming to terms with the fact that you can't have anything real together. I'm sure this is his way of trying to get you to let go."

"I don't intend to hold on to him."

"But how do you think he feels about you? He's told

me himself he loves you. Believe me, he never cared about me a tenth as much. But I know he was very, very sorry he ever caused me a minute's worth of pain. It was only inevitable. There can't be a happy ending to this, Katie. Surely you see that.''

Katie twisted her hands in her lap. ''I do see it. I guess I didn't want to think about it, though. I just wanted to take one day at a time, and hope that somehow——''

''Somehow you could find a way to be together? How likely is that? Don't you want a real man? Someone you can snuggle up with in bed at night? Someone who can accompany you wherever you need, or want, to go? Someone who can some day give you children?''

Katie was silent. ''Yes,'' she said, at last. ''Of course I do. I want all those things.''

''Then if this is Derry's way of trying to make it easier on you, and on him, maybe you could try to accept it. We're assuming he's stuck here. But what if there's a way to set him free? Don't you want him to go on?''

Katie shrugged miserably. ''Mary, you're right. Of course I do. I wouldn't want him not to have a chance to leave this place—pleasant as it is.''

''It's pleasant for you and me and anyone else who can leave when they choose. I wouldn't want to be stuck in those woods and on that beach for eternity, would you?''

In spite of herself, Katie laughed. ''Of course not.''

Mary patted her knee, then took a deep breath. ''You know that I've been doing a lot of reading lately. I have friends, too, who agree with me that there may be a possibility of interrupting the energy that flows through here, at some of its weaker points. So what I wanted to let you know was that we are planning to try and hold it back, and at least allow the possibility for Derry to escape.''

''And he'd be free.''

''Yes.''

''And gone.''

''Yes.''

Their eyes met and held for a long moment. ''I know that's best. When will you do this?''

''In a week and a day. We must wait for the darkest time of the moon. Catherine—that's my friend who's quite knowledgeable about such things—believes that there must be the least possible interference from other outside energy sources as possible. Are you upset with me for arranging this? I'll understand if you are.''

Katie shrugged. ''That wouldn't make sense, would it? I know that it's best for Derry to be free. You know a lot more about such things than I do. I only want what's best for him. No, I'm not upset with you. I'm upset in general.''

''What will you do?''

''About the paper?'' Katie clasped her hands together over her knees and gazed out the window. ''I was thinking of abandoning the project altogether. But I have to believe that you're right. I can see why Derry would do such a thing, especially if he thought there might be a way to leave soon.'' She sighed. ''It isn't fair to him to allow Alistair to publish such terrible things about him. If someone doesn't dispute Alistair, Derry will be branded a traitor and a spy. People will just accept what Alistair says. I mean, Derry's really just a footnote in history. Once there's a plausible explanation offered, I doubt anyone will take the time and trouble to investigate it further.'' Her eyes filled with unexpected tears, and she swallowed hard. "I feel as though I owe Derry that much, at least."

"What about the Prosers?"

"Oh, I can handle that, I think. I've already talked to Daphne Hughes. She's going to help me do some of the research, and my sister's boyfriend in Ireland is going to collaborate with me. So I'll have ways of keeping the heat off me."

Mary drained her mug. "That's wise."

"If you—um—if you should see Derry, please tell him that I understand."

Mary sighed. She gave Katie a sad smile and nodded in the direction of the woods. "I think he'll know. And I think that when he does, he'll not only be grateful, but he'll admire your courage."

Katie met Mary's eyes with a sad smile of her own. "I'll hope so. It's the best good-bye I can think of to give him."

As Mary walked through the woods, she gradually became aware of Derry beside her.

"How is she?" he asked quietly.

"As well as you can expect anyone to be," Mary answered. "She's upset. Your treatment didn't exactly help, you know."

He made an agonized sound that could have been a groan. "What would you have me do, Mary? You tell me to back away, to leave her alone? What should I have said? She'd have ignored the truth."

Mary paused, considering. "You're right. She would have. Perhaps it's best this way."

He muttered a curse beneath his breath. "I cannot see how."

Mary stopped in midstep and closed her eyes. "I'm too tired to go through it all again with you, Derry. I've spoken with Catherine and we're arranging the ritual in eight days. But do Katie a favor and let her get used to the idea of being without you, all right?" In the fading light, she could just about make out his eyes, and the sharp angles of his face seemed to make him look like a death's mask. She shuddered in spite of herself.

He turned away and spoke in a bitter voice. "As you say, Mary. I know you're right. It may tear my soul apart, but by the fate that binds me here, I know you're right." He faded into the cold twilight, and Mary closed her eyes and murmured a silent prayer for his ultimate rest.

Chapter Nineteen

The next few days passed in a haze of hurt. Katie felt as though she sleepwalked through the days, going through the motions of acting out her life. And at night, she collapsed into a heavy sleep, from which she rose as if drugged. Mercifully there was no sign of Derry, either in her waking moments or in her dreams. It was as if he'd simply removed himself from her existence. Which, she realized glumly after nearly a week with no contact whatsoever, was exactly what he'd done.

She had a desultory conversation with Patrick Ryan, but without her enthusiasm, she knew the project would lag. Daphne called and left several messages, but she couldn't bring herself to return the woman's calls. She was tempted more than once to call Meg, and unburden herself long distance. But the thought of trying to explain the events of the last month and a half to her sister, let alone the complicated emotions that were tearing her heart apart, seemed too exhausting a proposition.

She forced herself not to stand for hours and stare out the window into the woods on the other side of the pond. But all her waking hours were haunted by the siren song of the Stones within the forest, and she found herself pacing restlessly from room to room, only her pride preventing her from seeking him out.

Nearly a week went by, and each day that passed seemed like one more lump in her heart. Each day brought her closer to the day when the possibility of ever seeing Derry again would end forever. One evening, after class, she made a cup of tea and lay down on the couch. Her head ached and her eyes felt as though coins had been taped to the lids. She covered herself with her patchwork afghan and dozed.

He was kissing her, his mouth warm and sweet and tender, and his strong arms embraced her, wrapping around her, holding her close. Nothing existed except the sensation of his mouth on hers, his body on hers. She gave herself up to it, relaxing totally, and together they floated in soft haze.

Finally he pulled away, and she looked up into his eyes, eyes so deep a blue, she felt as though she could drown in their depths forever. "Forgive me," he murmured. "Forgive me for sending you away."

"Derry, I love you," she sobbed. "It hurts so much—"

"I know, I know." He soothed her hair back from her temples. "But it's the only way, careen. We cannot be together—eternity stands between us. I would give my soul to spare your hurt. . . ." He hesitated, then crushed her close. Longing washed over and through her like a

wave, and she clung to him, exalting in the certainty
that he did love her.

Katie opened her eyes. His presence gently faded, but
the feeling of love, strong and certain and real, stayed
with her. She glanced at the books piled haphazardly on
the coffee table. If they couldn't be together, she could
at least make certain that his name wasn't sullied. She
threw back the afghan. It was time to stop mooning
about and get to work. She dug into the notes she'd
made during her conversations with Derry. She quickly
typed an E-mail to Patrick, careful to include every scrap
of information she'd managed to glean so far.

She bit her lip and inwardly berated herself for not
taking better notes. She should have had the presence of
mind to review the notes immediately after she'd talked
to him, and made sure that she'd included everything
he'd said. But she hadn't thought that there could have
been a limit to the time they'd spend together. She hit
the ''send'' button and sat back, her arms folded over
her chest.

She had just picked her pen to begin outlining the
project when the telephone rang. She was surprised to
hear Patrick Ryan's voice. ''Pat!'' she said. ''Don't you
two ever sleep?'' At once, the implicit innuendo of what
she'd said hit home, and she blushed.

He only laughed softly. ''Only when we need it.'' He
paused, and then said, ''I read your E-mail. There's a
lot of information there, if we can prove it.''

''I was thinking diaries or journals. What do you
think?''

''I think it's a possibility, at least for the ones who
were members of the gentry. But more than half of these

men weren't much more than peasants. They probably couldn't read, let alone write.''

''Well, let's start with the most likely. Let's just split the list in half, shall we?''

''Sounds fine to me. You'll pop me an E-mail in a day or two?''

''Absolutely.'' As soon as she'd hung up, Katie grabbed her pen and made a list. She'd swing by the town library tomorrow on her way into class, and see how Daphne was coming. Hopefully, she'd know in a day or so which documents and materials would be difficult to find. At least it was a place to start. She glanced up and around the room. Derry's presence had faded, but despite the absence of any sense that he was close, she spoke aloud. ''You see, my dear Derry, we can make a difference for each other. And we will.''

A late-afternoon squall lashed against the windows of the classroom as Katie paused in her reading and looked up. Twenty pairs of sleepy eyes looked back at her. She had to bite her lip to keep from laughing. The expressions on the faces of these eighteen and nineteen-year-olds were the same as the ones her little brother used to wear when he'd wake up from his nap. She sighed softly. The most merciful thing would be to dismiss them all and assign them just that. A nap. Tucked inside her bag was the latest message from Daphne Hughes that most of her inquiries had borne fruit. An early dismissal would mean she could stop at the library and still get home before dark. Daphne must have been working night and day on the project, like a bloodhound on the chase, to accomplish so much in so little time. It was nearly the middle of October, and Katie was getting nervous. The January fifteenth deadline was looming ever closer.

But instead she said, "All right. Now that we've re-examined some of the language Freiere uses on the last couple of pages, what do you think he means by that passage?"

There was a slow stir in the rows. It rippled over the class like a shallow wave as students turned their heads one way or another, glimpsing to see if their friends and peers dared an answer. Predictably, with practically the same precision as a flock of birds, they turned back to gaze at her.

Oh, no, thought Katie, *I'm not bailing the lot of you out this time.* "Well, now, let's look at it another way. . . ." Her words were interrupted by the slam of the door. She looked around to see Alistair Proser leaning into the classroom, wearing a furious expression. "Alistair?" she blurted.

"May I see you a moment, Miss Coyle?" His voice was icy.

"Sure. Class, take another look at that passage, all right? Try to come up with an answer by the time I come back." She hopped off the edge of the desk where she'd been perched and followed Alistair into the hall. She shut the classroom door behind her. He led her a little way down the long, polished corridor. "What's this about, Alistair?"

"I think you should tell me what this is about." He thrust a note under her nose.

Katie took the paper and scanned it. It was a request from the university library to return a book. A book that she, through Daphne, had just requested. "What's your point, Alistair?"

"Are you going to deny that you're behind this request?"

Thinking furiously, Katie said, "Why would you think it's me?"

"All of a sudden a lot of requests have come into our library for books that have a direct bearing on my Clancy paper."

"I still don't see why you think it's me, or if there'd be a problem if it were."

"If I find out you're behind this, Katherine Coyle, things will go very badly for you here."

Katie drew herself up. "Are you threatening me, Alistair?"

His face was flushed and his eyes glittered dangerously. A vein throbbed in his forehead. "I don't make threats," he spat through clenched teeth. "I make promises." He turned on his heel and strode away, leaving her both shaking and puzzled.

She stood for a long moment, listening to his footsteps fade down the steps at the end of the hall. She considered whether or not to report this incident to Terry Callahan. She didn't want to seem like a goody-goody, she thought. But on the other hand, Alistair hadn't seemed just angry or upset. He'd been enraged.

"Katie?" The hesitant voice of one of the students shattered her reverie.

"I'm coming, Colin," she replied. "Just tell everyone class is over for today. We'll continue on Monday."

"Sure thing." He grinned and pushed the door further open.

She waited until the last of the students had left the room, most of them wishing her a good weekend as they passed. She gathered her things together slowly. The rain was even heavier now, and the sky was so dark, it looked several hours later than it actually was. She glanced at the clock above the door. Not quite four o'clock. She'd stop by Terry's office and just see if he was there. If not, she'd forget the incident.

She made her way to the administrative wing of the building and paused in front of the heavy oak door. A discreet brass plate announced his name. Through the frosted glass pane she could see lights blazing. *Oh, well,* she thought. *Maybe it's just the secretary.*

She pushed open the door and stepped from the polished linoleum floor onto a thick Oriental carpet. A woman with iron-gray hair and a pink cardigan around her shoulders glanced over the half glasses perched on the tip of her nose. "Yes? May I help you?"

"I'm Katie Coyle, one of the instructors in the English Department. Is—is Terry in?"

"Yes, he is. Would you like to speak to him?"

"If he has a minute, and it's not too much trouble."

"I'll see." The woman picked up the phone and spoke softly into the receiver. She looked back up at Katie with surprise. "He said to go right in." She nodded at the door to the left of her desk.

Katie eased open the inner door. "Terry?"

"Come in, come in!" he said, rising to his feet as she entered. "I'm so glad you took me up on my invitation to stop by. Come sit down. Would you like some coffee? How about a cup of tea on a gray autumn day?"

"Tea would be great." Katie looked around the large office. Despite its size, it still managed to have an air of coziness.

"Two Earl Greys," Terry said into the phone. "Now tell me, how *are* things going?" He steepled his fingers just below his chin and peered at her with all the benign interest of an academic Santa.

"Well," Katie said, trying to collect her thoughts, "things have been going pretty well—but something happened this afternoon, which I thought I should come and discuss with you."

"Oh?" He leaned forward and then looked up as the door opened and the secretary entered carrying a tray laden with cups, a sugar bowl and a small pitcher. "Just put everything right there, Doris. Thanks." He got up and picked up a mug. "Milk? Sugar?"

"Just a little milk, thanks."

He stirred two heaping teaspoons into his, then settled behind the desk. "Now. What's on your mind?"

"Just this afternoon, during class, Alistair Proser stuck his head into the classroom—"

"While you were teaching?" Terry frowned.

"Yes. I was very surprised, but even more so when I went out to talk to him and he just about threatened me about a library book request."

"Threatened you? How?"

"It wasn't very specific—he just said I'd be sorry. The thing is, we're both applying for the same grant. I guess it's just academic rivalry. But—"

"Still, to imply that you'd be sorry in some way is pretty strong. Did he threaten you physically?"

"No, not at all." Katie took a sip of tea. "Maybe I was hasty in coming to you—"

"No, no, my dear. You did absolutely right." Terry sat back in his chair and gazed at the ceiling. "The question is, however, how to deal with it."

Katie said nothing.

Finally Terry raised his head. "I know you've had a

tough time of it with Reg Proser. But let me fill you in on a little secret. Reg is retiring in June. But that still doesn't address what to do about his son."

"No, it doesn't. Listen, there really isn't anything he can do to me."

"That's not the point, Katie. There're some things that can be tolerated in the name of academic rivalry, and some things that can't." He paused, and gave her a long measuring look. "Frankly, I was surprised to see you go off with him on Friday. He didn't seem to be your—ah—type."

Katie shrugged. "He's not. But I didn't see any harm—"

"Did you . . . him . . . how shall I put this delicately . . . reject him in any way?"

"Well, I made it clear that the only dessert he was getting was what was on the menu, if that's what you mean."

Terry chuckled, then looked serious. "Let me give this matter some thought. In the meantime, come to me immediately if you have any other encounters with Mr.—ah—Professor Proser."

They chatted a few more minutes, then Katie finished her tea and took her leave, explaining that she needed to visit the library before going home. Terry shook her hand and wagged a finger at her solemnly as he opened his office door. "And remember," he said, "come to me at once if there's any repeat of that episode."

"I promise, Terry. Thanks for the tea." With a smile and a nod to Doris, Katie stepped into the main corridor. She felt much better, although something made her look both ways before heading out the door. She remembered what Derry had called Alistair—an idiotic popinjay.

Somehow she thought Terry Callahan was more than a match for him.

Lightning flickered across the sky, and thunder rattled the panes in the windows. Katie looked up from her reading as the lights dimmed momentarily. She got up with a sigh and hunted in the kitchen for matches. It seemed like a good idea to be prepared in case the electricity went out.

She settled back on the couch and scanned the text. So far she'd found nothing that might present her with a lead. She scanned the notes of her conversations with Derry. There must have been something she'd missed, something she'd overlooked. The fact that she was not as familiar with this period wasn't helping, either.

She rested her head against the back of the couch. If only she could speak to Derry. But she had the feeling that the last time she'd dreamed of him had been his final good-bye. She closed her eyes and spoke aloud. "Derry, I know you don't want to see me any more. And I know you feel that's for the best for both of us. But I need your help if I'm going to keep Alistair from painting you as a traitor. You've got to help me one more time. There has to be something I didn't ask you— or something I've forgotten—or something more you can tell me. Please, Derry, if you're anywhere you can hear me, just give me one more name. One more clue."

Thunder crashed, and a crack of lightning split the night sky. Katie jumped. The thunder reverberated and her heart pounded, and she nearly missed the soft whisper. *Reynolds. Magan. Fitzgerald.*

She started, staring around the room. "Derry, is that you?" She thought she caught the barest trace of bay rum. She got up and went to the window, pulling her afghan around her shoulders. The lights flickered several times, and another flash of lightning forked above the trees. She backed away, remembering her father's admonishments to stay away from windows during thunderstorms. She looked around the room as she retreated back to the couch. She grabbed a pencil and wrote the names as quickly as she could. She looked longingly at her computer, but knew if she tried to send an E-mail in this weather, she could very well ruin the modem. Not only could she not afford to be without her computer, she relied too heavily on E-mail to keep in touch with Patrick. She picked up the receiver, but instead of a dial tone, all she heard was a static buzz. *Well, that's just great,* she thought as she settled on the couch once more. She grabbed a book and her notebook. She might as well see what she could find out about these names as long as there was nothing more to do.

"Reynolds? Magan?" Patrick's voice crackled alarmingly over the shaky connection. Although the sun was shining and the sky was a brilliant shade of autumn blue, the telephone still seemed as though it was suffering some effect from the storm of the previous night. "They were both informers. Reynolds, especially, was a close friend of Lord Edward Fitzgerald—he was one of the organizers of the rebellion, you know. I'll check and see what's available on him. He was a colonel in the United Irishmen's army."

"I think there might be some connection to Kilmartin, too," Katie said, speaking as slowly and distinctly as she could.

"He was very well-connected to the whole organization," Patrick agreed. "I'll get right on it and let you know as soon as I can if I find anything. All right?"

"Sounds great." Katie glanced at the clock as she hung up. She had just a couple of hours to review her notes before class. She'd stop at the library, too. They were very close, she knew it. She glanced out the window across the ponds. In the early-morning light, the surface of the water was as smooth as polished glass. *Thank you,* she said silently as she settled down to work.

A million stars peppered the sky like grains of sand scattered across black velvet, and the dark water pounded the pale beach with a relentless roar. The white-robed women stood in a circle, hands clasped, and the tall, dark-haired woman who was their leader raised her hands and began a low, keening chant. The orange flames of the bonfire in the center of the circle leapt higher as the wind blew harder and swept the woman's hood off her head. Her long, dark hair whipped around her head and her black eyes glittered in her pale face.

Hovering above the gathering in an invisible mist, Derry watched, fascinated as the women began to weave in a complicated dance, two steps clockwise, three steps back, their hands linked tightly. Mary stood opposite the dark-haired woman, Catherine. The other eleven were hidden from him, for the most part, by their hoods and long robes. The circle tightened as the chant grew louder.

Imperceptibly at first, then gradually more distinctly, Derry felt the change in the flow of the energy that swept over and through him. He felt the relentless tide lessen, the iron hold of the force that had kept him imprisoned for nearly two hundred years relax. His essence seemed to shift, to float more freely, and beneath him, the women shifted and moaned, their chant dissolving into a long, keening wail, the words lost within the chorus of voices that blended into one, unified sound.

Catherine raised her arms once more, and Derry felt the tremendous power that coursed through the woman. It was as if she had somehow reached into the very depths of the earth itself and had somehow drawn the energy up and into her very self. The orange light glowed with weird intensity and her voice broke through the monotone chant of the others. "Diarmuid O'Riordan!" she cried, and Derry felt himself jerked by the summons in her tone. "Diarmuid O'Riordan. The way is clear! The time is come! Your path is free to leave this plane! Seek your soul's release! Go in peace and find your rest! Your path is free—so mote it be!"

"So mote it be!" moaned the other women.

Drawn as he was to the call in the voice, Derry at first fought the pull, and then relaxed as she repeated the words.

Above him the stars blazed hotter as though each one were a tiny bonfire on a black beach, and the waves reared higher as though they would engulf the women. But Derry felt nothing more. His body floated, ever more weightless, as Catherine screamed her incantation once more. "Your path is free—so mote it be!"

"So mote it be!" the other women echoed, their steps beginning to falter.

"So mote it be!" cried Catherine once again.

Derry felt the shift once more, as the circle began to weaken. The women stumbled in the sand, their clasping hands pulling free of each other. The tremendous tide of energy was breaking the circle apart.

Derry coalesced within the circle, as Catherine screamed once more, this time in frustration, "So mote it be!" She opened her eyes and looked at him.

The other women halted and sagged against each other, their faces covered in sweat. Mary gave a sound that sounded like a moan. "Derry?"

At once he turned to her, and caught her as she nearly fell against him. "Mary, are you all right?"

"I'm fine," she gasped. "We'll all be fine in a minute. It's just—"

"It's just it didn't work," snapped Catherine.

Derry slowly straightened. "Why not?"

Catherine paused. In the flickering light of the flames, he could see that she was a good-looking woman—large, ample-bosomed; her long, dark hair falling in thick waves about her full, pale face. She was about Mary's age, he knew, but the firelight was kind, erasing all the tiny signs of age around her eyes and mouth. Only her stance, aggressive as no maid's could be, told him that she was a woman to be reckoned with. Her hands were on her hips as she glared at him, her eyes on the same level with his. If there ever were a goddess, thought Derry, surely she'd looked a great deal like Catherine Armstrong did at this moment.

"Why didn't it work?"

The other women were collapsing on the sand and were passing flasks among themselves, murmuring to each other.

"I'm not sure," she answered, more thoughtfully than Derry expected. She alone stood her ground, her eyes ranging around the circle.

"I could feel the energy change," said one woman, looking up at Catherine.

"So did I," chimed in another.

"Oh, we managed to hold the energy back," said Catherine. She gazed out into the ocean, then turned to give Derry an appraising stare. She ran her eyes up and down his body, as boldly as he might over a maid's. To his consternation, he felt himself blush. "Maybe it's just not your time."

"What are you talking about, Cat?" asked Mary from her place in the sand. "He's been dead nearly two hundred years."

To his utter horror, Catherine reached out and pinched his cheek. "He doesn't feel dead to me." She threw her head back and laughed as the other women echoed with soft guffaws. Then she stopped abruptly, and took another step closer, so that she stood nearly toe-to-toe with Derry. "Maybe it's just not your time."

"What do you mean?" asked Derry, holding his ground. This woman was used to intimidating men with her voracious, overwhelming sexuality. He could feel it smoldering in her, like a banked fire.

"I mean maybe you have things left to do. And maybe you have to do them in this body. . . ." She raised her hand once more and squeezed his upper arm, her fingers digging into the flesh in a hard caress. "Mmm." She smiled into his eyes.

Mary had risen to her feet and was standing next to him. "Like what, Catherine? What could he possibly have left to do? He hasn't been able to get off this beach in two hundred years."

"How should I know that?" retorted Catherine. "I'm a witch, not a prophet. But I know one thing—you should be gone. And you, my dear Mr. Riordan, are anything but.'' She shrugged. ''I'm sorry, Mary. We can try it again next year, goddess willing.''

Mary turned to Derry, confusion in her eyes. ''I don't understand it.''

He took her hand. ''I don't either, Mary. Maybe your friend is right. Maybe there's something left here for me to do after all.'' He raised his head and gazed in the direction of Pond House, where he could feel Katie lying fast asleep, curled beneath her covers. ''Or maybe there's someone keeping me here.'' He dropped Mary's hand and bowed. ''Ladies. I appreciate your help. My eternal thanks.''

''Wait!'' cried Catherine. ''Are you leaving us?''

''I have an appointment of most pressing urgency, ma'am. I beg your indulgence.'' He gave them his most courtly bow, and disappeared in the midst of girlish giggles.

Formless, timeless, Katie floated, drifting aimlessly through a soft, gray mist. And then, without warning, he was there, bending over her, scooping her up in his arms, and the mist dissolved in a hot, piercing burst of light, which glowed and shimmered. ''Derry?'' she breathed, puzzled by his presence. ''Have you come to say good-bye?''

''Never, my beloved, never. I will not leave you—I cannot leave you. I'm here with you forever.''

''Forever?'' she echoed, but he was kissing her, his mouth hard and hot and demanding, and waves of sensation swept through her, pulsing through her blood. She felt herself melting into him, dissolving into the urgency of his need, and she twined her fingers in his thick, dark hair and smiled as she gave herself utterly to his desire.

Chapter Twenty

"Phone message for you, Katie," Fran Garibaldi smiled as she stuck her head around Katie's battered office door. She fumbled in the pocket of her dress, and frowned. "Damn, I had it right here. . . ."

"Come in, Fran." Katie beckoned to the woman.

The woman sifted through the large stack of folders she held in one arm. "I could've sworn I stuck it right in my pocket—"

"Well, that's all right. Was it urgent?"

"No, but it was all the way from Ireland. I figured if it was important enough for someone to call you from across the Atlantic, at least I could bring it up to you. I knew you wouldn't stop in the office again until you were ready to leave for the day."

"Was it from my sister?"

"Oh, no. A gentleman. With the most delicious voice I've heard in a long time. Made this old maid's heart melt."

"About what time was it?"

"You were teaching your morning class, I guess, so about eleven?"

"Okay, thanks, Fran." Katie smiled. "I know who it is. Thanks for telling me."

"You're quite welcome." The woman turned to leave, pulling the door shut behind her.

"Wait, Fran," Katie said, quickly. "Was there any message?"

"Gracious, how silly of me. Yes, he sounded quite excited. But all he said was . . . he'd found Kilmartin." Fran hesitated. "Yes, that was it exactly. He found Kilmartin." She smiled broadly. "I hope that's a good thing?"

Katie grinned back with delight. She felt like leaping to her feet and hugging the woman. "Fran, I think that may be one of the best things I've heard in a long time."

She waited until she heard the woman's footsteps recede down the hall, then shut her door firmly. She dialed the long international number carefully, her finger shaking on the old-fashioned dial. When Patrick answered, she said eagerly, "You've found Kilmartin?"

"I can't guarantee it yet. I've got a couple more things to check and see if I can get some corroboration. But I found a court order from September 1799, ordering a group of convicts to Australia. And next to the names—some of the names—are the initials WRK. I think it's been assumed over the years that it stood for "work." But it could also mean the—"

"*Wild Rose of Kerry*," she finished.

"Exactly. And on the list, there's a name T. Kilmartin. Timothy O'Riordan of Kilmartin, it could be. The fact is, since the ship disappeared without a trace, who would've known?''

''But what about the Earl, himself?''

''This is as close as anyone's ever come to knowing for certain what happened to either one of the brothers. I've already got a hold on the Reynolds's papers. I'm going over to check them tomorrow. I'll tell you as soon as I know something.''

''What about the other names—Fitzgerald is Lord Edward, you think?''

''Most likely. He would've moved in the same circles as our chap. But it's worth checking again. Although it was a man named Magan who ultimately informed on Fitzgerald, the connection seems obvious.''

''All right,'' said Katie. ''I have an outline of the paper all done—I'm going to E-mail that to you as soon as I get home. I have some reading to do, as well.''

''Good work, then,'' said Patrick. ''Listen, would you please call your sister? She's very worried about you for some reason. I tell her she's just jealous because at this point I'm talking to you more than I'm talking to her—but she's so embroiled in her work right now, she's living at the library.''

''Sure,'' Katie smiled. ''When will she be home?''

''She's got to come home by midnight. The library closes then.''

''Well, how about if I call around then? Will I disturb you?''

''At this point, not hearing from you will be more disturbing.''

Katie hung up after reassuring him she would call. She knew she'd been neglecting her sister, and she hoped that a simple conversation would assure her that all was well. As well as it can be, she thought as a pang went through her. It wasn't easy missing Derry.

Brooding, she gathered her things together and started out the door. The lock on the door caught her eye. The wood was splintered. She paused and looked at it more closely. It almost looked as though someone had tried to force the lock out of the ancient wood. It was old and worn, but looked relatively intact. The doorframe was obviously constructed out of hard wood.

Katie looked around. Had someone tried to break into her office? Was it possible that Alistair would stoop so low? She gazed around the tiny, dusty space. *No,* she thought, *you're being ridiculous, Katie.* Next you'll be seeing monsters under your bed. *Well, why not?* said the wry little voice of her conscience. *You've already been seeing ghosts in the forest.*

The telephone rang just before midnight. Katie leapt off the couch, her book tumbling to the floor. She grabbed the phone. "Hello?"

"Katie, is that you?"

"Hi, Meggie, of course it is. How are you? What time is it? It can't be more than five-thirty in the morning over there. Why are you calling at this hour?"

"Are you all right?"

"Of course I'm all right—"

"Are you sure?"

"Of course, I'm sure—"

"I really mean it, Katie. Is there something you haven't told me?"

"About what?"

"About anything. I've had a bad feeling about you for the past three days, and last night I had the worst dream. It was terrible—scared me absolutely to death. Are you sure you aren't in any trouble?''

"I'm not in trouble at all, Meggie. What makes you think so?''

"I've just had a really bad feeling that something had happened to you, Katie. A really bad feeling. And then I had this dream just now—it woke me up in a cold sweat, and all I could think of was to call you and make sure you were okay.''

"Meggie, you're scaring me. What exactly did you dream?''

"I'm sorry. I don't mean to scare you. That's the trouble with dreams—it was just a lot of running and bad feelings, and you being in terrible danger. I've been so busy these last couple of weeks, I know I haven't been here when you've called, and I've been thinking about you so much—I guess I was just being silly. Hey, did Patrick tell you that things have heated up again with the Alistair Proser thing?''

"No." Katie swung her legs over the side of the couch and rested her chin in her hand. "What's going on?''

"The professor I told you about—he's filed a formal complaint. He's not letting this thing go. Your Mr. Alistair is going to have to come over here and answer some questions at an informal inquiry.''

"Really? No way." Katie sat back, digesting the information.

"Oh, yes. It's not a secret here at all. Everyone's talking about it. You haven't heard anything over there?''

"No—but Alistair isn't on the faculty here. I guess his father has managed to keep any hint of it from getting around.''

"Listen, now that I think of it, you better be careful about letting this guy know what you're up to. I hope you're taking some precautions about his finding out. His reputation is already in question. If he finds out that you and Patrick are planning to publish a rival paper—one that's almost definitely going to call his conclusions into question—he may not be so nice. He'll try to use whatever influence he has with his father to get you dismissed. Have you thought about that?"

Katie plucked at a loose thread in her afghan. "Yeah, yeah, I've thought about it. He's already accosted me. Threatened me, even."

"Threatened you? With what? Did you go to his father?"

"No, are you kidding? I went to the Dean." Quickly Katie outlined her conversation with Terry Callahan. "So I've let it be known that there's a potential problem. I trust Terry will deal with it."

"In the meantime, I hope I can trust that you aren't doing anything foolish or deliberately calling attention to all this."

"Of course I'm not."

"Good. 'Cause I've had a very bad feeling about you for the last three days. I don't want you to get fired, or worse."

"What would be worse than getting fired?"

"Bodily injury?"

"Oh, Meggie, don't be so melodramatic." Katie stared at the ceiling. "Although it did look as though maybe someone tried to force their way into my office—"

"Force their way into your office?" Meg shrieked. "Did you tell your friend the dean?"

"Well, no, not yet. I've been busy."

"Are you living in a dream world?" Meg gave a loud sigh. "I want you to promise me you'll call him first thing tomorrow, okay? Stop dreaming over there, Katie. This could be serious."

I haven't been dreaming, Katie wanted to say. *I've been pining away after a ghost.* She wondered, fleetingly, what Meg would say to that. But instead all she said was, "Please don't worry, Meggie. I'll call Terry first thing, I promise. Did Patrick get my E-mail?"

"I think so. Look, you take care, all right?"

After repeated reassurances, Katie finally got her sister off the phone. She sat for a long time thinking about the situation with Alistair. If it were indeed the case that a formal complaint had been filed with some sort of review body, Alistair might be a more serious threat than she'd initially imagined. The last thing he'd want is to have to answer to two challenges simultaneously. As she settled into bed, she caught a whiff of bay rum. *Don't miscount your sister's warning. Alistair Proser could be a desperate man.*

She turned on her side and switched off the light. "I'll speak to Terry Callahan in the morning. I promise!"

She thought she heard a soft chuckle as she drifted off to sleep.

True to her promise, she stopped by Terry Callahan's office before she even went to her office the next morning. She found Terry looking over some letters with Doris. "Good morning, Terry."

"Katie Coyle! Twice in a week!" the big man boomed. He gave her a measuring glance and gestured over his shoulder. "Go right in." Katie had just sat down when Terry closed the door. "What's up?"

"I'm not quite sure I even believe what I have to say. But it looked to me last night as though someone tried to break into my office."

"Break into your office? What makes you think so?"

"The wood around the lock looked gouged. As though someone had tried to stick a screwdriver or a knife into the frame."

Terry frowned, seemed about to speak, then hesitated. Finally he said, "You come with me." He strode out of his office, heading for the outer door. "Just leave those letters on my desk, Doris. I'll be back in a few."

"Where are we going?" asked Katie as she hastened to keep up with his long stride.

"To your office, of course. I want to see this for myself. It's not that I don't believe you, Katie," he continued as they pattered up the steps. "It's that this is very serious. If anyone has tried to break into your office, we have to take precautions." At the top of the steps, he paused. "Which one?"

"That one," Katie pointed as she started down the corridor. She stopped. The door was open. Sunshine was pouring out the door and pooling on the floor of the corridor, something that could only happen if the door was open. "The door's open."

"And you didn't leave it like that?"

She gestured with her bulging tote bag. "I haven't even been up here this morning."

He led her down the hall. Together they peered into the office. Papers and books were scattered everywhere, lying in haphazard heaps all over. The place was ransacked.

"Good God." Terry's face was grim. "All right,

come with me. Don't touch anything. Did you have anything valuable inside?''

''Not at all.'' Katie shook her head slowly, feeling a chill run down her spine. ''Notes for my classes. Reference books. Student essays.'' Thank God she kept her materials for the paper at home.

''Come on. We'll go down to Fran's office and call the police. Are you all right?''

''I'm fine,'' Katie said, swallowing hard.

In the stairwell, he paused. ''You know, Katie, that this could be difficult. I know what you told me the other day about Alistair Proser. But before you go making any accusations, we're going to have be very careful. It's not likely that a respected professor like Alistair is going to stoop to this. I think it's a lot more likely it's one of your own students. Or possibly just some frat-boy prank.''

Katie met his eyes. A fist seemed to close around her heart. Of course, she thought. She should have expected this. The old-boy ranks were going to close around Alistair. He might only be a visitor on campus, but his father had enough stature to ensure that he wasn't going to be the most immediate suspect. And his own international reputation was going to protect him, too, for a while at least. Although maybe when word got out that a formal complaint had been filed in Ireland, his word wasn't going to be sufficient. But that wasn't likely to happen overnight, even if she mentioned it herself. And she did intend to mention it. Privately to Terry Callahan, at least. And, she thought, if it had been Alistair who'd broken into the office, he couldn't have found any of her materials for the Clancy article. ''Sure, Terry. I understand. I won't say anything about Alistair.'' *Unless*

I'm asked if I've been threatened lately, she added silently.

"Good girl," he nodded approvingly. "We just have to handle the matter delicately, you understand. We can't go rushing off half cocked, making up accusations that won't hold water. Know what I mean?"

Sure I do, she thought. Silently she followed him down the stairs to the main office of the English Department, where Fran sat frowning at a computer screen while she typed with frightening speed on the keyboard. As they entered, she looked completely surprised to see Terry. "Dean Callahan!" She paused in her typing, looking even more mystified to see Katie standing beside him. "What can I do for you this morning?"

"Is Reg in?"

"No, not yet. He never comes in till one today. Is there something I can help you with?"

"This young lady's office was broken into last night. Books, papers, everything, all scattered around. You can call campus security."

"Oh, my dear!" Fran got to her feet. "Are you all right? Is anything missing?"

"We didn't look," Terry answered. "Best not to touch anything until the police arrive."

"Well, come leave your things in Dr. Proser's office," said Fran. She put an arm around Katie and clucked sympathetically. "What a terrible thing!"

The morning passed in a blur. After class, Katie was summoned to her office, while a two-man team of police went over the entire office thoroughly. After they'd left, she went with Terry Callahan to his office, where a man dressed in street clothes waited to interview her.

They went into Terry's office and shut the door. "I'm

Sergeant Murdoch. You're Dean Callahan? And Dr. Katherine Coyle?''

Katie nodded.

After taking her address and checking the spelling of her name, he closed his notebook and put it in the pocket of his glen-plaid blazer. "Did you notice that anything was missing, Dr. Coyle?"

"No," answered Katie. "There really wasn't anything of value in the office. But I haven't had a chance to check."

"It was mostly student essays, books, notes—things of that nature?"

"Yes," said Katie. "Nothing really valuable."

"Any of your students athletes, Dr. Coyle?"

Katie blinked, taken off guard by the unexpected question. "A few."

"How are they doing?"

Katie shrugged, trying to remember. "Well, like a lot of students who have to try and balance a demanding academic schedule with a demanding practice and game schedule, it can be tough."

The two men exchanged glances. "Any in danger of failing?" Sergeant Murdoch asked.

Katie glanced from the sergeant to Terry Callahan. It was very obvious where this was going. They were going to try and say that the break-in was the result of students. "No," she replied quietly, refusing to play along. "None are doing any worse than a C."

"I see. Can you think of any reason—other than a prank, or to change a grade—anyone would try and break into your office?"

Katie hesitated. "Only if they were looking for something."

"And what do you suppose they could be looking for?"

Katie glanced at Terry. She was tempted to tell the sergeant about Alistair's threats, about the rival paper, and her research, but suddenly she didn't feel as though she could trust Callahan. He might be more favorably inclined toward her since he'd hired her, but it would take a tremendous amount to move him to do anything that would overtly anger Proser. She sighed. Academic politics. "I can't really think of anything. Maybe money, maybe a grade."

The sergeant looked at Callahan, who shrugged. "We're having the lock of Katie's door replaced this afternoon. She'll have a chance to go in tomorrow and make sure there's nothing missing. In the meantime . . ."

"If you think of anything, Dr. Coyle, please give me a call." He fished inside the pocket of his blazer, and pulled out a card. "Here. You can reach me with that beeper number. Give me a call any time."

"Thanks, Tom." Terry got to his feet. "Katie here was a little shaken by the whole experience. I wanted her to feel comfortable that we were doing everything to discover why this was done."

But not who did it, Katie thought. Murdoch rose as well, just as there was a knock at the door. "Come in," called Callahan.

Doris peered around the door. "There's a long-distance call from Ireland for Miss Coyle."

"Oh," said Katie. "Tell the person I'll call her back."

"It's a man," Doris said with a faint air of disapproval. "A Mr. Ryan."

"I'll call Mr. Ryan from home."

Doris shut the door. There was a round of handshakes and reassurances, and after Murdoch was gone, Katie gathered her own things. "I appreciate everything, Terry," she said as he escorted her to the main door of the building.

"You're not to worry about anything, you hear? Just leave all of that to us. I'll be speaking to Reg Proser later this evening. Don't forget to stop by and see Fran tomorrow first thing. She'll have your new key all ready."

"Thanks, Terry." Katie shook his hand and made her way across the lawn to the faculty parking lot. She heaved a huge sigh of exhaustion. It had been a stressful day. She was tempted to call Mary or stop by Mary's house on her way back to Pond House, but she was so tired, all she wanted was a hot bath and a cup of warm milk.

She glanced at her bag, and realized she had to stop at the library on her way home. She knew there was at least one book that Daphne had ordered for her. It wouldn't be fair not to stop and get it. The woman was working so hard for her, she'd have to send Daphne some flowers when this was all over.

She walked into the library and was surprised to see that Daphne was nowhere in sight. Her bell wasn't on the desk, either. How odd, thought Katie. She glanced around the corner into Daphne's office. The door was closed, but through the glass panel, she could see Daphne sitting behind her desk, her face pale, John Sneed bending over her, with a glass of water in his hand.

"Daphne?" Katie knocked gently, peering through the glass.

"Oh, Katie!" Daphne beckoned through the glass. "Come in!" Katie opened the door, puzzled by how relieved the woman sounded. "I'm so glad you're here. Come sit for a minute."

Katie glanced at John Sneed. The big man was standing over Daphne almost protectively, like a guardian angel. "What's wrong, Daphne? Are you all right? Are you sick?"

"Oh, no, no. I'm fine. Or I will be. That dreadful boy was here—he's not a boy anymore, not really, but I can never think of him as anything but that pampered little Lord Fauntleroy—" She broke off and waved her hand at John Sneed. "Go put my bell out on the desk, will you, John?"

The man nodded silently at Katie and went to do Daphne's bidding. When the door was shut behind him, Daphne leaned forward and put her head in her hands. "That dreadful boy." She looked at Katie. "You know who I mean. Alistair. Alistair Proser."

"He was here?" A chill went down Katie's back.

"Yes. Just a little while ago. He came in screaming about books—apparently he's the one who's got the books you've been requesting, and you were right about one thing—he certainly doesn't want to part with them at all!"

"What did he say to you?"

"He demanded to know who was asking for them. I tried telling him it was none of his business, and then he started raving about some Irishman. Someone named Reardon? Rordon? Something like that—anyway, he was just hysterical. And he grabbed the slip and saw your name—" Daphne broke off, looking distressed. "I tried calling you at the college, but I couldn't get an answer. The department secretary said she didn't know when you'd be in. And I left a message at your house—Katie, I think the man is crazy!''

"What did he do when he saw my name?''

"Stormed out of here. Didn't say a word, actually. I saw him drive off in the direction of the college. No wonder you wanted things kept quiet. I never saw such behavior in my life. And in a library, too!''

"Daphne, I'm really sorry. I truly am. I had no idea Alistair would behave so . . .''

"So crazy?'' Daphne shook her head. "It was a revelation to me, let me tell you. If he were my son, I wouldn't care how much of a big shot he was at Yale. I'd spank him and send him to bed without supper. Goodness!''

Katie repressed a smile. Somehow, she didn't think that punishment would be effective. "If it's not too much trouble, I came to get the books.''

"Of course. Come with me.'' She stood up and beckoned for Katie to follow her. She reached beneath the circulation desk and gave Katie the small stack of books. They had been bound together with a large rubber band. Katie's name was clearly written on an index card on top. Inwardly, Katie groaned.

"Thanks very much, Daphne. I'll—uh—I'll speak to Alistair if I see him. He shouldn't have acted that way at all.''

"You be careful, Katie Coyle. That man looked like he was ready to shoot someone.'' Daphne wagged her finger at Katie and leaned on the desk. "Just be careful. There's no paper in the world so important that anyone needs to get that worked up!''

Katie nodded in agreement and drove home slowly in

the quiet afternoon. There was no sign of Alistair anywhere. *Now what?* she wondered. Should she go back to Terry Callahan? What was it going to take before he'd believe her? Or what would it take to convince him to talk to Proser about his son?

She pulled into the driveway just as the late-afternoon light was filtering through the nearly bare trees. She parked the car and walked around the house to the front door. She fitted the key in the lock. For the first time since she'd moved in, the key stuck. She jiggled it in the door, and finally the door swung open.

"Katie!" She heard Derry shout across the pond, and turned to look at him in amazement. He was waving his arms at her. "Katie!"

She smiled at him as her heart leapt in her chest. She hadn't thought she'd see him ever again in the flesh, only perhaps in dreams. She waved back.

"Katie," he called again. "Don't go in the house!"

"What?" she called back, just as the phone began to ring.

"Don't—"

His words were lost as she stepped through the front door and grabbed the phone on the fifth ring. "Hello?"

"Katie, it's me, Patrick. I tried to get you at the college, and I know they said you'd call me, but I couldn't wait."

"What is it?" she asked breathlessly, sitting down. She saw Derry pacing along the periphery of the forest, pausing now and again to stare at the house with a grim expression.

"Reynolds, Fitzgerald, Magan—that was the breakthrough we were looking for. It must have been a piece of inspiration on your part, because there's no way I would've connected the three, except for Fitzgerald, of course. Magan was a double agent all along. I found this in Reynold's diaries. By putting it side by side with Fitzgerald, I was able to piece most of it together. There's a letter in Magan's papers, written by Timothy Kilmartin from Aix-en-Provence in May of 1800. He went to the Continent, not knowing that Magan was an agent. And he never got on that ship.''

''Which means that Diarmuid O'Riordan did, in his place.''

''Yes. That's my theory, too. The brothers switched places. Timothy had a wife and a child in the spring of 1798 when the whole thing fell to pieces. His brother had no one.''

''So the Earl died in the shipwreck.''

''Yes, exactly.''

Get out now, Katie. Derry's voice thundered in her head, and she gasped. *Get out now.*

''Are you all right?'' Patrick was asking.

''I'm fine—listen, I just walked in the door. This is all great news and I'm so glad you called to tell me—'' *Get out now, Katie Coyle! Now!* She slammed the receiver down and bolted to her feet, just as Alistair Proser stepped out of the hallway, carrying a gun. Katie gasped, and felt the blood drain from her face. ''Alistair?''

''Excellent sleuthing, Dr. Coyle.'' He gestured with the gun. ''Why don't you just hand over all the materials you've managed to piece together on the Earl of Kilmartin, and we'll just forget that this unfortunate little episode ever took place. I'll even forget to mention it to my father, who's itching for an excuse to fire you.''

''He can't fire me,'' Katie declared.

Alistair laughed. "Of course he can fire you. He can fire you any time at all within the first six months of your employment for any reason at all."

"There's no law against researching a topic for a grant."

"Do you think he's going to look very kindly on your stealing my idea?"

"I didn't steal your idea! The conclusions I've reached have nothing to do with you."

He shrugged. "Are you sure you'd like to risk him buying that one?" He gave a little snort. "I didn't think so. Now. Why don't you just give me all the books and all the notes, and anything else you might have managed to collect on the Earl, and we'll just forget all this. And thanks a lot for giving me the information I needed to solve the mystery."

"At least this will be one paper you won't be called upon to defend, right?"

His face turned bright red, and the vein throbbed in his forehead. "How did you know—"

"My sister's in Dublin. Remember?"

His face flushed an even deeper shade of red. "Give me the notes."

Run, Katie. Run to the Stones.

Instinctively she turned and ran out the door before Alistair could react. She heard him shout a curse after her. Heart pounding, she raced as fast as she could over the footbridge, where Derry stood waiting. He grabbed her arm and pulled her along beside him. Together they crashed through the trees, Alistair in hot pursuit.

Within the Stones, Derry pushed her behind one of them and stood in the center of the clearing to confront Alistair. He burst into the middle, his face flushed, twigs and bits of leaves in his hair, still brandishing his gun. "I want those notes," he roared.

"Easy, man," said Derry.

"You!" Alistair pointed the pistol at Derry and fired. Derry ducked behind a Stone while Katie shuddered.

"You can't win this, man. Put the gun down and go away. Leave Miss Coyle alone."

"And let her ruin everything I've ever worked to achieve? Not likely."

Katie could hear Alistair moving cautiously through the leaves that covered the grass. If she could work her way back to the path, she might be able to get to the house and dial 9-1-1 before he could catch her. She dodged behind the next Stone. Alistair whirled and fired again. The bullet ricocheted off the Stone and buried itself in a tree trunk. Katie cringed. Maybe she'd be better off staying put.

There was a rush as Derry tackled Alistair. The two men grappled and the gun discharged again, just as Derry knocked it out of Alistair's hand. "Grab it, Katie," he called.

Alistair swung at Derry and connected with his cheek. There was the sickening crack of bone hitting bone, and a cut opened. Blood poured down Derry's face. Katie reached for the gun, searching through the leaves. Alistair grabbed her by the waist and pulled her away, hurling her with a madman's strength to the opposite side of the Stones. She hit the ground heavily and cried out as Derry wrapped his arms around Alistair and rammed his head against a Stone. "Run, Katie! Call the police!"

Katie picked herself up. The world tilted and spun, and she staggered. Out of the corner of her eye, she saw

Alistair pick up the gun again. She took off down the path. There was another gunshot, and a blinding pain made her stumble. She fell to her knees, realizing that Alistair had shot her in the leg.

She heard Derry swear. He leapt at Alistair with renewed fury, bringing him down with one mighty blow. Alistair managed to fire one more bullet before Derry knocked the gun out of his hand. It flew in the air and disappeared among the trees. Derry hit Alistair again and again until the other man collapsed, unconscious.

Katie moaned. Derry ran to her side, picking her up in his arms. She placed her head against his shoulder. She felt rather than saw the sticky red stain that was spreading across his shoulder. "Derry," she managed. "You're hurt."

"Shh. 'Tis no matter to me. You're hurt, too. Here, I'll carry you as far as I can." He started off through the forest and she closed her eyes as nausea from the pain threatened to overwhelm her. Blackness descended on her like a whirling well. The last thing she heard was Derry's voice from somewhere high above, calling what could only be her name.

When she opened her eyes, she was lying on the couch in the living room at Pond House. A man wearing a medical technician's uniform was bending over her and a woman was taking her pulse. She started to sit up, and saw Derry seated in her desk chair. Another technician was binding his shoulder and a uniformed policeman was taking notes. Outside the door, she could see two more policeman talking to Sergeant Murdoch.

"Easy, miss," said the woman. "You've lost some blood. We're going to take you both to the hospital, but we wanted to make sure you were stable.''

"I—I'm fine,'' Katie managed. She looked at Derry. "Derry?'' she whispered. "You—you're here?''

"And it's lucky that I am, Katie,'' he replied quickly, meeting her eyes with a meaningful look. "We'll talk about this later.''

Sergeant Murdoch walked into the house. "Dr. Coyle. You're going to be all right. We've got Mr. Proser in custody. I've got men out there now, looking for the gun.''

"He admitted he shot us?''

"Oh, not at all. But it's pretty obvious to me that someone shot the two of you. And he's the only one without a gunshot wound, although someone''—here he looked at Derry—"certainly managed to inflict quite a bit of damage on his own.''

There was a stir outside, and Mary Monahan burst through the open door. "My God, it's true,'' she blurted when she saw Derry sitting bare-chested in the chair. "I—I couldn't believe—''

"Believe it, Mary,'' he said with a wide grin, sending her the same look he'd given Katie. "We can talk it all out later.''

"Absolutely,'' said the medical technician. He shut his bag and checked Katie's temporary bandage. "Let's get you both to the hospital.''

"I'll be coming by to take a statement from you, Dr. Coyle, after all the fuss is over. All right?''

"Sure,'' said Katie. There was still an unbelievable air to the whole thing.

"I'll—uh—I'll bring some clothes to the hospital for you, Derry,'' said Mary as the medical technicians brought in a stretcher.

"Thanks," he said with a grin. "In all the excitement, I seem to have lost my shoes."

Much later, Derry, Katie and Mary sat around a fire in the living room at Pond House, open cartons of Chinese food before them, Katie's leg propped up on pillows. The painkillers they'd given her at the hospital were doing their job.

Mary pushed her plate away with a sigh. "I can't explain it, you two. I've no idea what happened. The only thing I can think of, Derry, is that you weren't really quite as dead as you appeared. Or maybe hanging out in all the energy from the Stones somehow altered things for you."

"Or maybe," he said quietly, looking at Katie's face, "Maybe even the fates couldn't let us be parted once more."

Mary looked from one of them to the other. "Maybe," she said. Her voice was soft and the expression on her face was sad. She got to her feet. "I ought to get going. I'll stop in tomorrow and see how you're doing. Do you need anything before I go?"

"I'll be fine," Katie said, holding out her hand. "We'll both be fine. Thanks for everything, Mary."

She squeezed Katie's hand. "You're very welcome. Don't get up, either of you. I can let myself out."

When she had gone, Derry settled next to Katie with a sigh. She tentatively reached out and caressed his thick, black curls. He picked up her hand and pressed a kiss into its palm. "I can't believe this, Derry."

He turned to her and his expression was at once solemn and merry. "Believe it, Katie Coyle."

"How are we ever going to explain who you are?"

"An unexpected guest from Ireland?"

"It isn't that simple, Derry. There're things like visas and passports and social security numbers—" She broke off as he pressed his mouth on hers in a gentle kiss. "They'll deport you."

"That would be a bad thing," he said, gazing into her eyes.

"Unless, of course, I married you. You could stay here if I did that."

"That would be a very kind thing." He kissed the tip of her nose.

"Could you do that?"

For an answer, he gathered her carefully in his arms and cradled her head against his uninjured shoulder. "Katie, my love, I've waited two hundred years to do just that."

She snuggled close and sighed. The smell of baking bread filled the air, and in the fireplace, the flames danced higher. The wind whistled in the chimney with a low, keening moan. Derry looked up. "Hush now, you old house. We're all home, at last."

Epilogue

A gentle mist was falling as Katie and Derry climbed out of the little rented car onto the side of the narrow Irish road. They paused a moment, and Katie watched as Derry looked around. She stuffed the keys in the pocket of her jeans. Although he was rapidly adapting to life in the twentieth century, driving a car was something he hadn't yet tackled. She'd been a bit nervous to drive so far on the opposite side of the road, but their trip to Ireland wouldn't seem complete without a visit to Derry's ancestral home. It seemed only right that they should come here.

The road curved up and over a gentle rise, bordered with low stone fences, overlooking fields of emerald green. The mist caressed their faces, and the grass grew lush and thick at their feet. Cows grazed on the hills. "Do you recognize any of this?" she asked softly, loathe to interrupt his thoughts.

He shrugged and shook his head before answering. "There were more trees," he said at last. "It all looks so—bare."

"The forests were cut down for the wood," she said quietly.

A pained look crossed his face as he gazed over the landscape.

"Shall we go on to the village?" she said, after another long silence. "Or do you want to find the Stones?"

"I'd like to see the Stones," he replied. "It seems sort of fitting, don't you think? In a way, it's what began it all."

He held out his hand, and together they climbed over the low stone fence and tramped across the field. On a slight rise, beyond a small stand of spindly trees, the Stones rose gray and somehow twisted, as though the weight of the years had battered them out of their original shapes. They walked up the little hill until they stood within the inner circle.

"How amazing," Katie breathed, brushing a hesitant hand over the rough surface. "Old Ronan really did copy them, just as Mary said."

Derry merely nodded. He went from Stone to Stone, gazing at each one as though making its reacquaintance. When at last he completed the circuit, he came up behind her and wrapped his arms around her. Together they gazed out over the rolling Irish landscape. He buried his lips in her hair and she wrapped her arms over his, drawing him close. "What are you thinking?" she asked at last.

He heaved a deep sigh. "That it's been so many miles and so many years since last I stood here. And that the last time I was here—in this very spot—Annie was in my arms, just as you are now.''

"I'm so sorry," Katie whispered. "You've lost so much. . . ."

"Hush." His Irish accent had thickened in the week since their arrival, and the word was a caress. "I have you now. And that's enough—more than enough, Katie Coyle. Don't you ever doubt it." He reached down and pressed a kiss on her cheek, and she smiled in response. "If it weren't for you—"

"You might still be on that beach," she said in a light, teasing tone.

"Indeed."

They stood a few more minutes, staring out over the green landscape while the mist fell and the cows lazily munched their way through the thick grass. Katie leaned her head against his chest. So much had changed in the last few months. Alistair Proser had been convicted of aggravated assault and was serving time in prison, and Reginald Proser had decided to take an early retirement shortly after his son's conviction. Her parents approved of Derry, and even Meg had liked him immediately. A double wedding was planned for August. And she and Patrick Ryan had won the Clancy grant.

"We should go," Derry said suddenly.

"I think Kilmartin is just a few minutes up the road," she said. "It shouldn't be any problem to find."

He shook his head and pressed his cheek against her hair. "No, let's just go back to Dublin."

"Without seeing Kilmartin?" She turned to face him. "Surely you want to see it, don't you? The award dinner doesn't start until eight—we have plenty of time. It's not even two o'clock yet."

He gave her a sad smile and brushed a finger against her cheek. "I don't think I need to see how much things have changed here, Katie. It's funny, because so much of what my brother and Annie wanted to accomplish has been achieved. But in the process, everything I knew, everything that made this place seem like home has been lost. I'm not sure I know how to explain it." He shoved his hands into the pockets of his jeans and paced to the outer perimeter of the Stones. "Oh, this is still Ireland, and still as beautiful in some ways as I remember it. Surely there's no other place in the world so lush and so green. But it's not—"

"It's not the place you knew," she finished for him. "It's not really home anymore."

"No," he said. He drew a deep breath and squared his shoulders as he turned to face her. "I realized it as soon as I got off the plane, and coming here has only made it clearer. My home is with you." He opened his arms and she went to meet him. She buried her face in the damp wool of his light-blue sweater, a shade she'd picked because it so exactly matched his eyes, while he enfolded her in a strong embrace. "You're my love, and my future, and all that I am or will be is part and parcel of who you are, Katie Coyle. And that's quite enough. I reckon I've been given more than any other man."

She drew back and gave him a long look, but at last she nodded. "All right. If you're sure. We can always drive out this way tomorrow or the next day, if you want."

"I know." He bent and kissed the tip of her nose. "Come." He held out his hand. "I can't wait to see you and Patrick receive that award."

"It should be yours," she teased. "You are, after all, the Missing Earl. In the flesh."

He chuckled. "I'm afraid you'd be accused of the same sort of thing as our Mr. Alistair."

"Fabricating evidence?"

"Inventing source documents."

They laughed together as they made their way down the hill and through the field to the car. Derry climbed into the passenger side without another look, but Katie paused once more to gaze at the grassy pastures. This was the only Ireland she had ever known, an Ireland far more settled than anything Derry could even envision. But it would always be the place that had given her everything that had ever mattered. Including Derry. She grinned to herself and slipped inside the car, fumbling for the keys.

"All ready to receive the adulation of your adoring public?"

"As long as you'll be there, too." Katie turned the key and the ignition sputtered into life. "You're as much of the public as I care about."

"There's nowhere else I can even imagine wanting to be," he answered. He picked up her hand and pressed a kiss into its palm. "Come on, Katie. Let's get this over with, so we can go home."

"You really don't think of this as home?" she asked curiously, as she turned the car around on the narrow lane and headed back toward Dublin.

"After two hundred years?" He shook his head. "The only home I need is the one I share with you." They exchanged another smile. Katie tightened her grip on the steering wheel. She pressed her foot on the gas, and the little car leapt forward into the misty afternoon.

Friends Romance

Can a man come between friends?

❏ **A TASTE OF HONEY**

by DeWanna Pace   0-515-12387-0

❏ **WHERE THE HEART IS**

by Sheridon Smythe   0-515-12412-5

❏ **LONG WAY HOME**

by Wendy Corsi Staub   0-515-12440-0

All books $5.99

Presenting all-new romances—featuring ghostly heroes and heroines and the passions they inspire.

❤ Haunting Hearts ❤

❑ *A SPIRITED SEDUCTION*
  by Casey Claybourne   0-515-12066-9/$5.99

❑ *STARDUST OF YESTERDAY*
  by Lynn Kurland   0-515-11839-7/$6.50

❑ *A GHOST OF A CHANCE*
  by Casey Claybourne   0-515-11857-5/$5.99

❑ *ETERNAL VOWS*
  by Alice Alfonsi   0-515-12002-2/$5.99

❑ *ETERNAL LOVE*
  by Alice Alfonsi   0-515-12207-6/$5.99

❑ *ARRANGED IN HEAVEN*
  by Sara Jarrod   0-515-12275-0/$5.99

TIME PASSAGES